The Missing Duchess

The Missing Duchess

An Inspector Faro Mystery

Alanna Knight

G.K. Hall & Co. • Chivers Press
Thorndike, Maine USA   Bath, Avon, England

This Large Print edition is published by G.K. Hall & Co., USA and by Chivers Press, England.

Published in 1996 in the U.S. by arrangement with Curtis Brown UK.

Published in 1996 in the U.K. by arrangement with Macmillan General Books.

U.S. Softcover   0-7838-1650-2   (Paperback Collection Edition)
U.K. Hardcover   0-7451-4849-2   (Chivers Large Print)
U.K. Softcover   0-7451-4852-2   (Camden Large Print)

G.K. Hall Large Print Paperback Collection.

The text of this Large Print edition is unabridged.
Other aspects of the book may vary from the original edition.

Set in 16 pt. News Plantin by Warren Doersam.

Printed in the United States on permanent paper.

British Library Cataloguing in Publication Data available

Library of Congress Cataloging in Publication Data

Knight, Alanna.
  The missing duchess : an Inspector Faro mystery / Alanna Knight.
      p. cm.
    ISBN 0-7838-1650-2 (lg. print : sc)
    1. Faro, Jeremy (Fictitious character) — Fiction. 2. Police — England — London — Fiction. 3. Large type books. I. Title.
  [PR6061.N45M57   1996]
  823'.914—dc20   96-2272

For
Dick and Elizabeth Warfel
and the magic of Cockleshell Cottage,
East Lothian

Chapter 1

The discovery of a woman's body in the Wizard's House in the West Bow was a sombre end to what had been an unusually convivial evening for Detective Inspector Jeremy Faro.

The Annual Regimental Dinner in Edinburgh Castle had provided everything to his taste; victuals excellent, drams in constant supply, toasts short and witty. But the highlight of the occasion was his reunion after many years with his cousin Leslie Faro Godwin.

The war correspondent was guest of honour. That in itself was something of a novelty where newspapermen were still regarded by the rich and famous with suspicion. Jackals of society, who earned a contemptible living by scandal-mongering and exposing the shortcomings of their betters for the titillation of their readers.

'Gentlemen sometimes wrote for the press, but newsmen were rarely gentlemen.'

Whoever penned that sneering epithet had never encountered Leslie Faro Godwin, thought Faro proudly as he listened to his cousin's talk. Leslie, who was five years his senior, was the veteran of many campaigns. Brave as any soldier, utterly fearless, he had 'lived in the cannon's mouth', as he described it, for twenty years and

7

made light of his imprisonment and torture by the late Emperor Theodore of Abyssinia during the early years of the war which had ended in 1868. After eight years of dodging Maori spears in New Zealand and Ashanti spears in Africa, he had recently returned from covering military operations in the Malay Peninsula.

The evening's entertainment left scant opportunity for private conversation between the two men. As they dived for shelter from the heavy rain to await their carriages, Godwin shouted:

'Edinburgh weather never changes, that's for sure.'

'It can be relied upon to be totally unreliable,' said Faro as they shook the moisture off their evening capes.

Godwin regarded him with satisfaction. 'Good to see you after all these years, Jeremy. You're quite a celebrity.' He chuckled. 'Hardly surprising really. You had a very enquiring turn of mind, even as a small child.'

'I appreciate your delicacy. Some called it just plain nosey!'

'Perhaps, but it paid off. You certainly fulfilled your early promise.'

'And so did you to all accounts.'

Faro glanced at his cousin approvingly. Experiences calculated to turn most men's hair white overnight, had not even flecked with grey his thick dark hair and splendid military moustache. Difficult, Faro thought, to label him as past forty.

'It has been a very long time,' said Godwin,

evening, sir. Constable Reid, sir.'

'What's the trouble?'

'Laddie here taking shelter from the storm found a woman's body in the Wizard's House.'

'The Wizard's House.' Godwin nudged Faro. 'How appropriate for a sinister discovery.'

'I've sent for the police doctor. Glad you're here, sir,' he added gratefully. 'Perhaps you would care —'

'Very well, Constable,' said Faro. 'Don't wait,' he added to Godwin. 'This may take some time.'

Faro stepped out of the carriage reluctantly. He had his own personal reasons for hating the West Bow. It was just yards away, where the West Bow joined the High Street, that his policeman father had been killed by a runaway carriage forty years ago.

Now stumbling into the unlit house on the heels of the Constable and the lad, whose name was Sandy, Faro's scalp prickled with that primeval sense of unease, of being in the presence of death.

The Wizard's House, as Weir's Land was commonly known, had a bad reputation. Empty for years, the passage of two centuries had failed to dispel the aura of evil left by its one-time owner Major Weir, warlock extraordinary, burnt at the stake in 1670.

Inside the house, along a narrow passage a high-windowed room provided enough light to reveal what looked like a bundle of rags but was in fact a woman lying as if asleep on the floor.

'Let's _ve s_ light,' Faro said irritably. 'Turn _ _e la__. Are there no candles?' he added __era_

Cons__ _ F_ smiled wryly as he held the lantern _h_

'Doe_ _ to make much difference, sir. And we _a_ _et candles to stay alight.'

'Wha_ d_ _u mean?'

'They _e_ _lowing out, Inspector, that's what.' He lool_d _und anxiously. 'As if someone was standin_ ri_t behind them,' he added, managing, at Faro_s _ern glance, to turn an uneasy laugh into a _ _gh of embarrassment.

'Yo_ _houldn't believe everything you read, Const__e.'

'It'_ _ gey uncanny place though, Inspector. And _m not given to being fanciful.'

F__ could believe that. Constable Reid was a n_ _ recruit from Glasgow, nineteen and tough as _l_ boots.

_le bent over the body. A beggar-woman in a _our ragged gown. He wasn't very good at guess-_g women's ages, but she looked youngish, not _uch past thirty. At least there was no blood, _no signs of violence.

'Any means of identification?'

'Nothing obvious, sir. Except that life is extinct. I know that is all I have to establish — before the doctor comes —'

'Quite right, quite right, Constable,' said Faro.

He found himself wishing that Vince had been with him, that he didn't have to touch the corpse himself. He pushed aside a quantity of soft fair hair and laid his hand on the cold flesh of her neck. There was no pulse.

'Some poor unfortunate by the look of her. May I join you?'

Turning, Faro found Godwin looking over his shoulder. His surprise at the request must have shown, for his cousin sighed.

'You never get used to it, do you?'

Faro shook his head, grateful for his understanding. If there was one thing more distasteful than the discovery of a corpse it was one without any means of identification. In his book, that always spelt trouble.

'Wait until you've seen as many as I have, Jeremy, and not neat and tidy as this one.' Leslie paused and added apologetically: 'I hope I'm not intruding.'

'Of course not.'

Godwin nodded. 'This is not just morbid curiosity, I assure you. First lesson for any newsman worth his salt is never to miss any opportunity. A corpse and a wizard's house, well, there's sure to be a story in it somewhere, at least a couple of paragraphs,' he added cheerfully.

As they regarded the body, which Faro realized had probably been dead for several hours, he could see that the lad Sandy was becoming restive. Hopes of the reward his chums had urged might be in the offing if he informed the dreaded 'polis', were fast fading. The appearance of Inspector Faro and the other gentry on the scene in their

15

evening finery, replaced such heady prospects with less pleasant possibilities. They might ask him questions, lock him up in a cell.

Shifting from one foot to the other, he announced with determined regularity that he wanted home. 'I only found her, your worships. I never done nothing.'

Constable Reid drew Faro aside. 'Shall we let him go?'

'I think that would be in order. Get his name and address, though.'

Gratefully, Sandy stammered out the information and bolted from the scene, his hand tightly grasping the shilling that the gentleman had given him plus an extra penny and instructions to summon a carriage. His tornado-like exit almost swept Dr Cranley, portly and majestic as a ship in full-sail, off balance.

The police surgeon's examination was brief: 'Natural causes. Massive heart attack, I'd say. Vagrant, taking shelter, no doubt; although she looks uncommon well-fed,' he added.

As he straightened up, regarding the fetid dark room of death with disgust, the stark contrast of men in evening dress surrounding the corpse struck Faro anew.

'What makes you think she was a vagrant?'

Cranley regarded him irritably. He knew Inspector Faro's reputation but he was already late for a supper engagement and intended to be out of this vile hole as speedily as possible. Death he was used to, but he feared for his elegant clothes where every movement produced an acrid cloud of dust.

'Look at her rags. Filthy. Nothing underneath either,' he added primly, hastily adjusting the ragged skirt he had lifted to reveal a bare thigh. 'Fallen on bad times, I expect, usual story. We'll do a complete post-mortem when we get her to the mortuary. Ah, here they are, at last. You've taken your time,' he added impatiently as two constables bearing a stretcher stumbled along the narrow passage.

Reproached for their tardiness, they explained that they had been delayed at Leith by an 'incident'.

Followed in solemn procession by the living, the dead woman was carried out to the police carriage. Under the flickering lamplight Faro tucked one of her limp hands beneath the rough blanket.

His quick glance confirmed Cranley's diagnosis that she had indeed fallen on bad times. And very recently too. The last resort of starving women who possessed such splendid hair was to sell it to the wig-makers. But like her hair, her fingernails were not only clean but well-grown and neatly manicured, her palms uncalloused.

These were hands that had not seen anything resembling hard work in a very long time. If ever.

Undoubtedly a lady's hands.

Chapter 2

At 9 Sheridan Place — the home Faro shared with his stepson — Dr Vincent Laurie, newly elected treasurer of the local golf club, was wrestling with his predecessor's accounts. He was therefore only mildly interested in his stepfather's encounter with a long-lost cousin, especially since he knew of Godwin's family connection and had nothing but contempt for their neglect of widowed Mary Faro and her young son.

Vince prided himself on being a man of the people and the Godwins belonged to the social system that had branded him illegitimate after his mother, a fifteen-year-old servant, had been seduced and abandoned by a noble guest in the big house where she worked. Even though she had eventually regained respectability through marriage to Jeremy Faro, such scars were burned indelibly into Vince's soul.

'The family's behaviour wasn't Leslie's fault, Vince. He was just a child at the time.'

'Then why has it taken him so long to track you down, Stepfather? Answer me that.'

'He's been abroad for years,' said Faro defensively, with an added reason for wishing Vince to think well of his cousin.

'I'm not convinced.'

'You will be when you know him better. I'm sure of that. If you'd been with us last night —'

As he went on to describe the scene in the Wizard's House, Vince paid careful attention. Eyeing his stepfather shrewdly, he said:

'I take it you disagree with Dr Cranley's verdict that death was from natural causes.'

Faro shrugged. 'I'm not sure. But let's just say, this was no beggar-woman.'

'No doubt your "missing persons" will provide a satisfactory explanation.'

On the list Faro consulted in the Central Office the following morning, there was no one who fitted the description of the dead woman in the mortuary.

Dr Cranley stared at him resentfully over the tops of his spectacles. Detective Inspector Faro's appearance signalled that the routine the police surgeon endeavoured to keep as smooth and untroubled as was humanly possible could be in imminent danger of severe disruption.

Faro regarded the sheeted figure. 'Any marks of violence?'

'Only a bruised and swollen wrist. She had fallen quite heavily. My findings have confirmed that she died of a massive heart attack.'

'Surely that's unusual in a woman so young,' said Faro. In death, there remained an indefinable look of refinement about that waxen face.

Cranley shrugged. 'Heart failure can happen at any age, Faro. And I would speculate, it is not all that unusual in the case of a protected and pampered middle-class woman who is suddenly subjected to direst poverty.'

Faro sighed, his attention again drawn to clean hair, to delicate hands with long tapering fingers and neatly manicured nails. They worried him.

'What makes you so sure she was middle class?'

Cranley sighed, drew back the sheet. 'Observe the narrowness of her waist, the distorted line of bosom and hips. I would say that she was richly corseted for most of her adult life. You don't get that shape among the poorer classes, Inspector.'

'So what would make this one become a beggar?'

The doctor eyed him pityingly. 'Many things, Inspector. Family scandal, for a start. Bankruptcy. A faithless lover — or a straying husband —'

'I suspect this lady, whatever her station in life, was unmarried.'

'Indeed?'

'Observe the third finger of her left hand. Married women tend to bear marks of a thick wedding ring, the skin it covers is paler due to lack of exposure.'

'Of course, you are probably right.' Cranley smiled thinly. It was a matter of constant irritation to him that Inspector Faro usually was right. 'We will no doubt find that out when her identity is established. Incidentally, she is not virgo intacta, but she has never borne a child. That we do know.'

In the days that followed, Faro went about his routine work at the Central Office praying that there would be no major crisis while Superintendent McIntosh was away attending a family funeral in Caithness. Sergeant Danny McQuinn, who Faro had learned to rely on, was also absent, seconded to Aberdeen on a murder enquiry.

Rifling through the new reports each day, he noted with relief that the Queen was safely tucked away in Balmoral Castle, absorbed by visitors for the last of the autumn shoot.

There had been a flurry of anxiety when unconfirmed rumour hinted that she might be contemplating a brief private visit to the Palace of Holyroodhouse. Even such unpublicized Royal one-day visits were calculated to give Edinburgh City Police nightmares. Tight security measures and extra police duties were only a small part of the expenses involved in the protection of a monarch whose popularity had steadily declined during her long widowhood.

Faro sighed. He hoped that Her Majesty would change her mind. She frequently did.

As for the newspapers, they had been having a field day. With no sensational crimes for some time, they were quite overjoyed at any item calculated to raise their sales.

'Body found in Wizard's House. A Third Tragedy. Is Major Weir's ancient curse still active? Does his evil spirit still malevolently guard his ancient abode of magic, seeking to avert the threat which hangs over the future of the historic West Bow?'

For some time, the Edinburgh Improvement Commission had been urging that the West Bow be demolished to make room for more salubrious modern dwellings.

'Especially,' they argued, 'as the evil reputation of Major Weir's house has caused it to remain empty for the most part of two hundred years, and has made even the poorest families shrink from sheltering under its roof.'

However, even when fears of witchcraft and black magic began to disperse in the more benevolent wake of the Age of Reason, and Major Weir's house was regarded with less terror by neighbours, all attempts at finding a tenant with strong enough nerves to inhabit it, failed miserably.

Some fifty years earlier, in the 1820s, William Patullo, an old soldier of reprobate and drunken habits, moved in with his wife. They moved out again the next day after a terrifying ordeal in which it seemed that all the powers of hell had been loosed upon them. As they spread the story of their discomfort far and wide, the shades of superstitious terror closed in once more.

In more recent years, the house had served as a gunsmith's shop. The business had failed for not even a shopkeeper could stay for long.

Undeniably, two deaths and an accident had followed the Improvement Commission's decision but they could hardly be classed as tragedies. The first death could not have come as a surprise. The demolition contractor was a man in his eighties, who breathed his last in his own bed, surrounded by his devoted and weeping family.

Even Detective Inspector Faro would have been hard-pressed to find anything remotely suspicious in such a peaceful end. Especially after a talk with the family physician, a golfing friend of Vince's who had expected his long-ailing patient to expire several years earlier. The funeral over, the eldest son who had inherited the business fell on the turnpike stair and broke his leg.

An unfortunate accident but hardly classifiable as 'a second tragedy'. The second death, however — the unidentified corpse of a beggar-woman — breathed new life into the old terrors and superstitions.

The press, hungry for sensational news items, were not unhappy at this resurrection. ('What fearful sight had stopped her heart and brought about this untimely end?') As they dusted down and reprinted once again details of Major Weir's infamous life, Edinburgh citizens shuddered and took to the other side of the road to avoid the menacing shadow cast by the newspaper-designated 'house of death'.

When Faro was handed the Procurator-fiscal's report with the police surgeon's usual request for an 'unidentified and unclaimed' corpse, his questions were once again greeted with a certain lack of enthusiasm.

'I can find no evidence of anything other than heart failure,' Dr Cranley told him.

'You are quite satisfied with the post-mortem?'

'If I wasn't, Inspector, then I would hardly be making this request. I regret having to disappoint you,' Dr Cranley added heavily.

'I think "disappoint" is an inappropriate word, doctor.'

Dr Cranley sniffed. 'Come now, Inspector. I realize with few murders on hand at the moment you must regard it as your duty to be on the look-out for anything remotely suspicious —'

'Let me assure you, sir,' Faro interrupted, 'murders are a commodity I could well do without. I don't invent them for my own amusement.'

Cranley smilingly dismissed Faro's protest and indicated the document on his desk. 'Then perhaps you would be so good as to sign this, Inspector, so that no more time might be lost.'

As Faro hesitated, Dr Cranley continued, 'I must urge you to be brisk about it. You surely realize more than most the value of this still-fresh corpse for my students. It is rare indeed that we get the chance of such an excellent unmarked specimen. One, in fact, with all the organs in prime condition —'

'Spare me the details, if you please.' Faro shuddered. 'I'll take your word for it,' he added, stretching out his hand for the paper.

The doctor, relieved, nodded happily. 'Then

I may take it that you are quite satisfied with our findings?'

Faro wasn't, but he could not think of one reason to justify his unease.

He tried to explain his feelings to Vince over supper that evening. Their meetings at meals were rarer than ever, since Vince held his surgery and consulting hours in the downstairs rooms. Fast acquiring a thriving practice, his leisure hours were increasingly devoted to reducing his handicap on the golf course.

'There are lots of reasons why an unmarried woman — thirtyish, you said — might have run away from a respectable middle-class life, Stepfather.'

'Tell me some of them.'

'An unhappy love affair — maybe hopes of marriage with a suitor over several years that had failed to materialize. Perhaps he married someone else and being jilted affected her mentally.'

Faro was disappointed, having hoped that his stepson would be able to come up with a more original selection of ideas than Dr Cranley had offered.

'A *Bride of Lammermoor* — is that what you have in mind?' Faro shook his head. 'Such situations belong in Sir Walter Scott's novels, Vince. Surely no sane woman —'

'No sane woman, Stepfather — ah, there's the rub,' said Vince triumphantly. 'For whatever the post-mortem revealed about her physical condition, it can tell us nothing of the state of her mind at the time of death.'

'Are you suggesting that what she died of was that condition known to ladies addicted to romantic novelettes as a broken heart?'

'Something like that.' Vince nodded eagerly. 'It can happen, you know. And the reason she was not on the missing persons file is easy. In all probability her wish to escape from the past brought her to Edinburgh from some other town or village.'

'It doesn't explain why a woman gently bred should feel obliged to change into a filthy beggar's gown. And what happened to her middle-class dress and her middleclass undergarments?'

'The answer is really quite simple, Stepfather. No doubt she had to sell them for food and lodging. Hunger can do incredible things to even the most fastidious.'

'This woman wasn't half-starved. I have Dr Cranley's word for that and the evidence of my own eyes.'

Vince shrugged. 'Perhaps she wished to shed her identity with the clothes.'

Faro looked at him. 'You are suggesting the utter destruction of self, of the woman she had been.'

'Something like that. There is another possibility. That whoever found her decided that it was a shame to waste good clothes when they could be sold.'

Faro thought of Sandy. 'I don't think the lad would have that much ingenuity. He seemed quite terrified to go near the body.'

Vince sighed. 'I should stop worrying about it, if I were you, Stepfather. Vagrants are ten a penny and every month some unfortunate falls to the students' dissecting knives. After all, we have to be practical about it. And once dead, the fresher the bodies the better for our purposes.'

'You make it sound like a flesher's shop,' Faro said accusingly.

'And so it is.' Vince eyed him candidly. 'All in the interests of medical science. Remember that one dead body dissected may lead to a hundred — perhaps a thousand — live ones being saved from the ravages of disease.'

Then almost eager to change the subject for he knew only too well what his stepfather was like once he got a bee in his bonnet, namely, an unidentified corpse in the police mortuary, Vince continued:

'But you wanted to ask me something about this newfound cousin.'

'I have invited him to dinner on Sunday. You will have your chance then to form your own impressions.'

Chapter 3

At their first meeting, when Faro had set down Leslie Godwin at the somewhat bleak lodging in the Lawnmarket, he had found himself thinking of his own comfortable house in Sheridan Place, run so smoothly by their housekeeper Mrs Brook, that model of efficiency. Guiltily, he had remembered the empty rooms upstairs and almost involuntarily this space had been filled with a satisfying picture of his cousin in temporary residence.

As the days had passed the idea grew in his mind. Faro had few relatives and Leslie was quite a find. A second successful meeting when he came to dinner and was very impressed by his surroundings confirmed that the two men had much in common.

Both had been subjected to danger from an early age, Leslie to wars, Faro to violent crime. Both knew how to deal with the unexpected, the art of survival perhaps an inheritance down the generations from that distant Viking ancestor.

Faro noticed with delight when Leslie dined with them that Sunday how Vince's air of reserve fast dissolved as the evening progressed and the talk veered from Leslie's recent progress as guest in the homes of Scottish nobility to his more exciting tales from the battlefield. Of how, confessing to the sketchiest of medical knowledge, acquired out of necessity, Godwin had used his own ingenuity and common sense to keep a seriously wounded prisoner alive until help arrived.

Faro, listening to the two men swapping medical experiences, decided that perhaps Godwin, who talked so cynically about taking enemy lives, was being excessively modest about those he had also saved.

The fact that Vince too was impressed by this relative reinforced the proposal Faro had in mind. He now felt certain that his stepson would approve of Godwin sharing their house during his short stay in Edinburgh.

Vince's reaction was exactly what he had hoped for.

'A capital idea, Stepfather. Let's ask him tomorrow night.'

Godwin, returning to his lodging the following evening, was clearly puzzled but pleasantly surprised to find the two of them waiting for him.

Faro had to put their proposal to him then and there, guessing by his cousin's nervous glances towards the window of his apartment as they talked that he was too embarrassed to invite them inside.

'My dear fellows. I'm grateful — touched even — by your kindness.' He shook his head. 'But I must decline. I am somewhat set in my ways, I've lived alone and lived rough, too long. It's no use trying to civilize me. I come and go and sleep and wake at all hours of the day and night. I couldn't put you and your excellent Mrs Brook to all that inconvenience. I'm much better off with my Sergeant Batey, he's served me faithfully for umpteen years and he's used to my ways.'

'He could come too. We have plenty of room in the attics.'

Godwin chuckled. 'You haven't met him yet. I guarantee he's as eccentric as his master, which suits us both well. He'd drive Mrs Brook — and you — mad. No — no — I couldn't think of inflicting us both on you.'

'We might persuade him yet,' said Vince as they walked home. 'Incidentally, we're invited to Aberlethie for the weekend. Terence and Sara are having a few guests.'

The weekend house party was popular among Edinburgh's rich and fashionable merchant class — those with mansions grand enough and gardens magnificent enough to allow gratifying illusions of rubbing shoulders with the aristocracy. And this was the society, Faro thought cynically, that Vince, self-declared man of the people, now moved in.

Sir Terence Lethie was one of his stepson's new golfing friends, and the proximity of a course to the castle suggested to Faro that he might have to make his own amusement.

Faro had a solid lack of interest in golf, he was immune to its fever, declaring that he spent enough time on his feet without regarding the pursuit of a golf ball across a green full of holes and aggravating hazards as an agreeable way of spending his leisure hours.

When he protested that he would be out of place in such an assembly, Vince smiled.

'Some of Lethie's Masonic friends have been invited. And Terence wants you to come specially, a guest of honour.' He coughed apologetically. 'He wants you to tell them about some of your cases.'

'So I'm to sing for my supper, is that it?'

Seeing his stepfather's expression, Vince said: 'I thought you wouldn't mind. And since you are so interested in local history you'll have a chance to meet Stuart Millar. He's a near neighbour.'

The local historian came of a famous family of travellers, one of whom had accompanied Sir James Bruce of Kinnaird on his travels in Abyssinia in the last century.

He was also a Grand Master in the Freemasons. Most of Vince's new acquaintances belonged to the order and Vince was being urged to join as an 'apprentice', the first rung on the ladder.

This was an invitation Faro had resisted personally for many years, despite Superintendent McIntosh's hints that 'it could do great things' for him. Although he refrained from saying so to his superior officer, Faro was happy to have reached his own particular niche in the Edinburgh City Police by his own merits, rather than by

31

joining what he regarded as an archaic secret society for ambitious men.

He was also content to remain Chief Detective Inspector, since the next step up that ladder would involve sitting behind a desk issuing orders and signing documents, work which he would find extremely dull after twenty years of chasing criminals and solving crimes by his own often unorthodox methods of observation and deduction.

'The Lethies are having some quite illustrious visitors,' Vince assured him. 'None other than the Grand Duchess of Luxoria, the Queen's god-daughter.'

Faro had read about Luxoria, one of the bewildering number of European principalities set adrift by the breakup of the Holy Roman Empire, its borders for ever under threat of annexation by other powerful states. But the tiny independent kingdom tucked away in central Europe had managed to survive centuries of warring and predatory neighbours.

He knew little of its complex politics since European history was not one of his interests, but he had been vaguely interested to read a legend connected with the Scottish Knights Templars, who had taken refuge there from persecution, rewarding the Luxorians with some holy relic brought from Jerusalem.

Luxoria might have remained in obscurity and never achieved even a small paragraph in the local newspaper but for the Scottish connection. The

Grand Duchess Amelie claimed descent not only from Mary Queen of Scots, but was related to both Her Majesty the Queen and the late Prince Consort.

'Didn't they have a revolution — oh, fifteen years ago? I seem to remember reading about it,' said Faro.

'Full marks, Stepfather. I had it all from Terence. The Grand Duchess inherited after her father's death. She was opposed by her wicked cousin, who had been set up, not against his will, as President and puppet ruler. She was then forced to marry him in what is to all accounts still a wretchedly feudal system of government.' Vince continued: 'A political marriage which would guarantee the succession and save further bloodshed. The Luxorians love their Royal Family, it seems, in spite of it all.'

At the thought of their own Royal Family, Faro smiled wryly. There were many disillusioned citizens in Scotland who applauded Ireland's demand for Home Rule. There were many others too in Britain generally who would have considered it a 'good thing' to bring down the Throne. The Queen was far from popular, spending most of her time in Balmoral Castle guarded by the fiercely protective John Brown, with only token appearances at the seat of government in London, to the dismay of her statesmen.

The French Revolution remained heavily in the forefront of men's minds. Less than a century old, others than the Luxorian Royal Family were feeling echoes of a drama that could still make princelings shake in their shoes. The secret files of the Edinburgh City Police held information concerning a tide of aristocratic refugees seeking sanctuary at the Palace of Holyroodhouse as privileged guests of Her Majesty.

On the eve of their departure for Aberlethie, Faro was summoned to Edinburgh Castle to investigate an attempted burglary. As he walked up the High Street from the Central Office along the West Bow, the bright moonlight and a sky wreathed in stars seemed to emphasize the sinister menace of the darkly shuttered Wizard's House.

Again Faro relived the child he had been, four years old, holding tightly to his weeping mother's hand as she took him on a pilgrimage past the spot where his father had died. Or had been murdered, as she maintained and as he was to prove beyond a shadow of doubt many years later.

At the Castle, Colonel Wrightson, who had entertained him so regally at the regimental dinner, was surprised to see him again.

'Good of you to come, Faro. I appreciate your personal interest.' He smiled. 'Surely this is rather low-key for you?'

'Not at all. Anything that happens on the outside of the castle walls is for the police. Once inside, then it's yours.'

There was little to see beyond a broken window and a displaced iron bar, but all suggested that the would-be intruder was a man of considerable strength as well as the possessor of a remarkable head for heights. It also hinted to Faro that this might be a situation worth keeping an eye on, a prelude to something even more dangerous.

When he said so, Wrightson smiled. 'I see from the newspapers' report that you had quite an interesting epilogue to your last evening with us. Another crime for you to solve.'

'Not this time, Colonel. Death was from natural causes. Some poor woman with a heart condition taking shelter.'

'I'm relieved to hear that. All these ridiculous stories about ghosts and ancient curses.' He sighed. 'They should spend a night here. That would set their imaginations going. Ghastly deeds in the Wizard's House indeed, they're nothing compared with the violence this castle has seen over the centuries.

'As for the Palace.' He sighed indicating Holyroodhouse, where he had been Captain of the Household Guard some ten years ago. 'It has an even worse reputation if that's possible. Rizzio's murder and God knows what other evil-doing. Yet I've spent many a night alone when the Queen wasn't in residence and I've never seen a single spectre. Lot of rubbish, if you ask me.'

Despite these reassurances, Faro was glad of the carriage the Colonel insisted on providing for him. As it made the tortuous steep descent of the West Bow, the horses' hooves striking sparks off the cobbles, the cloudless sky had vanished and a moon now trembled between clouds breathing life into the mullioned windows of the West Bow's ancient houses.

At one stage, the sergeant-driver reined in cursing, narrowly avoiding a closed carriage racing past at high speed. As they swayed dangerously, he heard the soldier shout:

'Not so much as a damned lantern. And black horses, too.'

Faro watched the carriage disappear, the sweating horses, their breath still on the night, the only evidence that this was no phantom coach.

A black carriage and black horses —

From the depths of memory loomed an almost remembered childhood nightmare that had engulfed his father and his beloved cousin Leslie.

The next instant he was faced with the unpleasant reality of the present. As the driver set their carriage to rights, there was an almighty crack as one wheel hit the high stone kerb.

Faro clambered out and shouted: 'What is it?'

The man was surveying the damage, swearing volubly. ' 'Fraid you'll need to wait till I fix this, sir.' And shaking his fist at the Wizard's House, towering above them, a vast black shadow:

'Aye, curse you too! Might have known it would happen here. Be a good thing when that damned place is pulled down.'

'I wouldn't have taken you for a superstitious man, Sergeant.'

'Not me. But my second cousin tried to live there once. You've probably read the story, it was in the newspapers. Ghosts and hobgoblins —' He looked up. 'An' he's not fanciful. Fought in the Crimea, he did —' The driver paused to kick the buckled wheel viciously. 'This is going to take some while, sir. You'll like enough pick up a hire at the stance down the High Street.'

Faro walked quickly away. Another accident in the making or just one more coincidence.

He looked back at the tall land and resolved that tomorrow with daylight on his side, he'd have a careful look round, carry out his own investigation and prove to Edinburgh's nervous citizens, and to himself, that Weir's Land was only wood and stone. As such it had no earthly powers to harm anyone except those who were gullible by nature and predisposed to place every misfortune at the door of superstition.

Tomorrow morning, however, was still several hours away.

In Sheridan Place, Vince was impatiently awaiting his return with a story of his own unpleasant encounter.

Chapter 4

Faro had failed to locate another carriage after the accident. Hardly surprising since it was past eleven o'clock, a time at which all respectable Edinburgh citizens were presumed to be in bed and asleep, especially by coachmen in foul weather. And the storm that had been threatening all evening now turned the full force of its attention upon the sleeping town.

Wind and rain fairly hurled Faro down the High Street and through the Pleasance to Newington where he unlocked his front door, very wet and in no very good mood, to find Vince far from sympathetic. Mrs Brook's excellent steak pie and treacle sponge pudding, Vince's particular favourites, had been ruined by his late arrival, to that good lady's distress and his own annoyance.

Following Faro to the kitchen, Vince watched as he peeled off his outer garments and spread them out to dry, Mrs Brook having retired some time earlier.

'You'll never credit this, Stepfather. I was called into Solomon's Tower to attend a visitor. Yes, you do well to look surprised, our Mad Bart had company.' And pausing dramatically, he pursed his lips. 'A lady.'

Sir Hedley Marsh, or the Mad Bart as he was

better known in the locality, lived in a crumbling sixteenth-century tower at the base of Arthur's Seat. A recluse, a woman-hater, this novel occurrence was of sufficient interest to take Faro's mind off his discomfort.

'Youngish and quite comely. Walking along where Samson's Ribs joins the road to Duddingston. And there was a landslide.'

'Not again, surely.' The exposed rockface known as Samson's Ribs could be dangerous, especially in bad weather when rocks and loose earth were dislodged with nothing to stop them falling on the road far below.

'We had complaints of a landslide quite recently. I thought they'd done something about it,' he added.

'You know what these authorities are like, Stepfather. No doubt they're waiting for a fatality and then the Improvement Commission will take action.'

'Tell me about this young lady. Was she badly hurt?'

'Nothing serious. Knocked off her feet, a few bruises. Not nearly as bad as it could have been, but she was very shocked, quite inarticulate. Kept weeping all the time.'

Vince shook his head. 'You know how the Mad Bart mumbles, but I got the gist of it. He had opened his front door and found her there sobbing and crying. Thought it was one of his cats in trouble. He didn't know what to do but wrap her in a blanket and go for help. And then, of

39

course, just as he was leaving: "There you were, young fellow, golf clubs and all," ' Vince mimicked with a grimace of distaste. 'Really, Stepfather, that dreadful old man —'

Faro, having dealt with wet clothes, now packed newspapers into his soaked boots to speed up the drying process. He only half-listened, with amused tolerance, to Vince's tirade. His stepson hated few people but Sir Hedley Marsh was one of them.

From their earliest days at Sheridan Place it seemed that Vince had found particular favour in the Mad Bart's eyes and Solomon's Tower was hard to avoid if they walked to Newington by the short cut through the Pleasance and Gibbet Lane.

As the Tower was adjacent to the more cheerful surroundings of the modern golf course, it had now become increasingly difficult for Vince to evade encounters with the aristocratic recluse.

'I would swear he sits by that window all day, though how he manages to see anything through the grime is a mystery. I now have to sidle past like a criminal, for if he sees me he rushes out, invites me in for a dram. A dram, in that squalor, surrounded by his infernal cats everywhere —'

Faro tried not to smile, for Vince, who could sit for hours reading quite contentedly with Mrs Brook's ginger cat Rusty purring like a kettle on his knee, entertained no such sentimental feelings about Sir Hedley's 'feline army', the innumerable stray cats he had given home to over the years.

'It's disgusting —'

'Come now, Vince, I consider that rather an admirable and endearing trait,' said Faro. 'Can't you see it as a pathetic gesture, an appeal for companionship from a lonely old man?'

'I can't see it, but I assure you, I can smell it. When he opens the door — really, Stepfather, the place should be condemned as a hazard to health. I could hardly breathe. That poor woman, too. I just hoped she wouldn't succumb to asphyxia before I did.'

Faro, who had been unfortunate enough to cross the threshold on several occasions, could only agree. Still, he did find Vince's animosity trying. He went on and on about it. Why on earth should he hate this tiresome but well-meaning old man? Such venom was quite out of character with Vince's normal serenity, his generous spirit.

'What happened to your patient?'

Vince shrugged. 'I left her there. Offered to see her safely home, of course. But she said no, she would prefer to rest a while. She did seem in rather a state,' he added, frowning. 'In the normal way, I would have insisted, but I just had to get out of that house. I had to breathe fresh air. He said he'd go out and get a carriage and I wasn't to worry. So I didn't,' he ended, closing his mouth defiantly.

Faro had been too preoccupied with getting dried and heating water to make himself a hot

41

toddy to feel sympathetic towards Vince's encounter with the Mad Bart.

Now when he mentioned his own unpleasant
near-accident with a runaway carriage that hurtled
out of the darkness, he was somewhat hurt by
Vince's merriment as any possibly sinister implications were mockingly dismissed.

'Really, Stepfather, it happens all the time.
After all, the West Bow's a threat to everyone,
the sooner it's pulled down the better.'

Glancing at Faro's solemn face, he smiled.
'Come now, you know as well as I do that carriages are positively uncontrollable there if the
cobblestones are wet or icy. You are lucky there
was no more damage than a buckled wheel —'

'And a long walk home on a very wet night,'
Faro put in acidly, seized by an uncontrollable
fit of sneezing.

Vince was unrepentant. He stretched out his
hand firmly. 'And I'll take some of that hot toddy
too, if you please. I could do with it, I can tell
you. After my experiences.'

Faro said no more. Bidding his stepson goodnight, he went grumpily up to bed where he fell
asleep to be haunted by bad dreams. Closed carriages drawn by wild black horses swept towards
him and ghostly lights appeared at the windows
of Major Weir's house, to a grisly accompaniment
of maniacal laughter.

As always, Vince's good temper was restored
by a night's sleep. The prospect of a weekend

42

house party at Lethie Castle with some decent golf pleased him no end.

The impending visit to Aberlethie had also caused a flurry of extra activity in Mrs Brook's kitchen, where the warm smell of baking battled with the aroma of hot irons and boot polish.

As the two men cautiously entered her domain, she beamed on them proudly. She did like her gentlemen being well cared for. A task she sometimes found extremely difficult since Inspector Faro cared not the slightest what he wore as long as it was clean, moderately tidy and comfortable, appropriately warm or cool according to the prevailing state of the weather.

Now to his disgust Faro was called upon to pay particular attention to sartorial matters, the choice of shirts and trousers, collars and cravats. At last the hour of departure dawned, the Lethie carriage arrived and they set off in some style with a proud Mrs Brook waving goodbye.

'And enough luggage behind us,' said Faro, 'to accommodate an entire family of grown-ups and children on a seaside holiday for a month.'

Aberlethie lay some twelve miles east of Edinburgh on the shore of the River Forth. It was a journey that, given the right weather, no traveller could fail to enjoy.

Faro, unused to such luxury, relaxed happily against the well-upholstered seats which smelt pleasantly of expensive cigars. The horses trotted briskly down twisting tree-lined roads and lanes, all with a splendid view across the estuary to the hills of Fife, following a coastline which had seen a fair share of Scotland's turbulent history.

Through Prestonpans, where Prince Charles Edward Stuart, victorious after battle, glimpsed through the mirage of destiny himself crowned king in Edinburgh. A mirage as false, alas, as the gold shimmer of the sandhills twisting through the bent grass by the shore. To their left the long white rollers moved in majestically to break in a gentle thunder upon the sandy beach. Above their heads the plaintive calls of seabirds, of curlew and sandpiper; while on the rocks seals raised their heads to stare lazily at the passersby.

Behind them a fast-retreating prospect of Arthur's Seat, a crouching lion rampant over Edinburgh Castle on its rock. Ahead of them, the skyline was now occupied by the glacial left-overs of Bass Rock and Berwick Law. Their more immediate horizons were obliterated by groves of sea buckthorns, those eldritch trees for ever leaning against the wind in attitudes of intense desolation which even the sunniest day refused to dispel.

This scene of melancholy was at last interrupted by the high gates and drive to a pleasing Georgian mansion which had replaced the original Lethie Castle.

Faro nodded approvingly. He found its clear and stately lines pleasing, preferring both his architecture and his lifestyle to be kept as simple and uncluttered as possible.

At his side, Vince smiled. He had long ago decided that his stepfather's everyday existence, dealing with the tortured minds of criminals, had influenced his aversion to the modern taste for Gothic architecture.

Climbing the front steps, they were met at the door by the butler and ushered up a grand oak staircase to their rooms.

While servants brought in his luggage, Faro stared into the rose garden below his window. One of the best views in the house, he decided, with its tranquil outlook over the once magnificent Cistercian priory, now reduced to a solitary ivy-clad wall.

Vince appeared at his shoulder and whistled appreciatively.

'You did better than me, Stepfather. I only overlook the front drive.'

Warm water and soft fleecy towels had been provided for their ablutions, and when Vince returned a little later, his stepfather was adjusting his cravat in the long mirror. Vince watched approvingly. For one who cared not a jot for how he looked or what he wore, Jeremy Faro would, as usual, be the most distinguished presence at the gathering downstairs.

Vince sighed, tugging at his own cravat and wishing he had chosen a different colour. It didn't seem quite fair that his handsome stepfather should have this inbuilt flair for what was right, without seemingly paying such matters the least attention.

'Shall we?' he said.

As they descended the stairs, the murmur of voices indicated the drawing-room where the Lethies already mingled with their guests.

Sir Terence and his wife Sara were an attractive, lively couple in their late-thirties. Sara was known to be bookish and a supporter of good works. A necessity, Faro suspected, since her husband spent a considerable time in London and when he was at Aberlethie was to be found mainly on the golf course.

They greeted Vince warmly and, Faro duly introduced, they were whisked in the direction of a group of men chatting near the window. There were no familiar faces for Faro. Most were his stepson's golfing acquaintances, and after the briefest and most perfunctory of greetings, Vince was speedily involved in the mysteries of handicaps and birdies, the tragedy of the rough and the language of the golf course.

Faro had no part in this, and neither apparently had the golfers' female partners who had long since withdrawn to the opposite side of the room and taken over two sofas where they chattered amiably on more domestic and social topics.

As Faro devoted himself to a study of the book-lined walls, he was addressed by a cheerful:

'Detective Inspector Faro, is it not?'

'It is.'

The tall white-haired man smiled, and the

rather anxious self-conscious look he darted towards the book Faro held, served as introduction.

'Mr Stuart Millar, I presume? I'm delighted to meet you.'

As they shook hands, Millar frowned. 'Have we met before, sir?'

Faro shook his head. 'I think not, sir.'

'Then how — ?'

As Millar, frowning, looked round the assembled guests, Faro said: 'Let me explain. You are the only gentleman present who is not absorbed by golfing matters. You are also, if I may say so, a little older. Your face and hands are deeply tanned, not with the transient Scottish summer tan which quickly fades but with the accumulation of many years of foreign travel. Also — may I —'

He took Millar's right hand. 'Your index finger is calloused, just here at the top joint, a frequent indication that a man spends much time with a pen in his hand. And last of all, I could not fail to notice that you recognized the book I'm holding as one of your own. Your latest, in fact, which I look forward to reading.'

Millar laughed. 'Well done, sir. And I guarantee it will appeal to you, for it is a kind of detective story. I have been looking for the clues that my grandfather hinted at when he accompanied James Bruce of Kinnaird on one of his expeditions to the source of the Nile in 1770.

'Bruce belonged to the minor Stirlingshire ar-

47

istocracy and inherited enough wealth to indulge a passion for foreign travel. He was something of an enigma, an eccentric we would call him, absorbed by the theory that the Jews in Abyssinia were descendants of King Solomon's misalliance with the Queen of Sheba which had resulted in a son, Prince Menelik.

'His research was meticulous, but my grandfather suspected there was a great deal more in his letters than scholarly research, which Mr Bruce for his own reasons did not wish to have published.'

Faro's interest in the goings-on of Old Testament worthies was somewhat limited and he could only smile politely as Millar went on:

'My grandfather's letters hint that Mr Bruce might have been on the track of a greater treasure.'

Pausing, he regarded Faro quizzically. 'In fact, you might find the Luck o' Lethie particularly interesting —'

Before he could say more, they were interrupted by the arrival of an attractive, vivacious woman with black curls and sparkling eyes. Petite, pretty and breathless, she took Millar's arm.

'Stuart, dear, aren't you going to introduce me?'

'Of course, my dear. My sister —'

Elspeth Stuart Millar, who Faro guessed was nearer his own age than her brother's, took his hand eagerly. 'You are a celebrity, Inspector Faro, and my brother is very naughty to monopolize you.'

Looking at Bruce's book which Millar held, she said: 'Do leave all your boring old theories at home, dear. I'm sure Mr Faro didn't come here to linger in the dust of past times.'

Transferring her hold to Faro's arm, she looked up into his face. A ravishing smile completed the picture of elegance and charm. 'Dear Stuart has a bee in his bonnet about our grandfather. I assure you, he was a most tiresome old man. And desperately mean, too —'

Millar gave a good-natured shrug as Faro, with an apologetic glance over his shoulder, allowed himself to be led away to a sofa by the window where Elspeth spread her skirts, and fan in hand, settled herself comfortably.

'There are so many things I'm just dying to ask you, Inspector. I know you won't probably be allowed to tell all. One has to be discreet —' She leaned forward confidentially. 'Do tell me, do you ever meet the dear Queen when she's at Holyrood?'

This was one of the questions most frequently addressed to Faro across dinner tables. His answer was a smile and vague nod and a refusal to be drawn into further discussion on the subject. He was well acquainted with Her Majesty and the Prime Minister. The people who questioned him would have been very impressed by such information.

But Elspeth Stuart Millar was quite right in her assumption. Such information was classed as 'highly confidential', for several times during his

49

years with the City Police he had been instrumental in averting disaster and Royal murders which would have changed for ever the path of British history.

Some day, in a distant future when all the main characters including Faro himself were part of history, no doubt those stories would be told.

'What is she really like, I mean? And er, is there any truth in those shocking stories about her behaviour with John Brown?'

Faro was saved further comment as turning, he saw Vince rushing towards them, his manner considerably agitated.

'Excuse me, madam.' And leading Faro away, he pointed. 'Over there, Stepfather. By the door —'

Chapter 5

Following Vince's anguished stare, Faro saw Sir Hedley Marsh standing in the doorway, blinking owlishly at the assembled guests.

As if still unable to believe his eyes, Vince murmured: 'The Mad Bart, Stepfather. What on earth is he doing here? Surely the Lethies never invited him!'

Faro shared his stepson's surprise. It was unknown for the aristocratic hermit to be lured out of Solomon's Tower to a social gathering.

'Dear God,' groaned Vince. 'If I'd seen the guest list, I'd have refused —'

But wonders weren't over by any means. As the Lethies went forward to greet him, from the shadows of the hall a young lady emerged.

At first Faro wondered if he was witnessing a manifestation of the family ghost in a dress of a bygone age.

'That's the woman I told you about,' Vince murmured. 'I didn't know this was to be fancy dress —'

Even though Faro's experience of female apparel was slight, he could see that the full skirt and *décolleté* neckline were reminiscent of the paintings of the young Queen Victoria on the walls of Holyroodhouse. The white silk of the gown had acquired the yellowish hue of age while the silk roses swirling across its skirts were faded blooms indeed.

As for the wearer, her face was as pale as the gown she wore. She was having considerable difficulties with the revealing neckline and a waistline that flowed rather than fitted. In fact the picture presented was of a garment whose original owner had been of shorter and more robust proportions.

As for the guests, they were too well-bred, too well-clad and in full control of any expressions of astonishment as their host and hostess led a shambling but reasonably clean and tidy Sir Hedley and his lady into the room.

'What on earth can Terence be thinking of? — Oh Lord, he's seen us.'

There was no chance of escape as Sir Hedley rushed forward and ignoring Faro, eagerly seized Vince's hands.

'My dear young fellow. What a pleasant surprise. If I had known you were to be here we could have shared a carriage. You remember — er — this young lady.'

As Vince bowed over his erstwhile patient's hands, a sudden smile banished her anxious and bewildered expression. 'Of course I remember you — the doctor. You were so kind.'

'And this is Dr Laurie's stepfather, Detective Inspector Faro. My — er — niece — Miss Marsh.'

At that extraordinary introduction, 'Miss Marsh' suddenly crumpled, clinging to Sir Hedley for support. She looked ready to faint and Vince sprang forward.

'May I sit for a moment, please,' she whispered.

Sara Lethie, aware that all was not well, came swiftly over and from her reticule produced the smelling salts which she wafted briskly under Miss Marsh's nose.

Eyelids fluttered open, regarded the faces staring down at her. 'Where am I? What has happened?'

'You are with friends, my dear,' said Sara. 'And this is Dr Laurie — And here is your uncle —'

'Uncle?' Miss Marsh stared up at Sir Hedley, who cleared his throat and murmured:

'Well, my dear, what a to-do.'

At that she closed her eyes hastily and leaned back against the sofa.

By this time the polite guests were stricken in poses of mild curiosity, heads craned in the direction of this interesting tableau.

Sara was mistress of the occasion. She was used to dealing with the vapours of her female friends. 'I think it would be best if Miss Marsh rested upstairs for a while. Come, my dear.'

'Allow me to assist you, Sara dear.' Elspeth Stuart Millar sprang forward and with Vince bringing up the rear, Sir Hedley's thoroughly improbable niece was escorted out of the room.

Faro watched them go followed by the curious glances and whispered speculations of the guests. The young woman was undeniably comely. Tall and willowy, with honey-blonde hair, Miss Marsh fitted admirably into that category Vince, so susceptible to female charms, in happier circumstances would have described as 'a stunner'.

At his side, Sir Hedley, aware of Faro's disbelieving expression, shuffled his feet and looked uncomfortable. 'Not really my niece, y'know. Can't remember her name. Lost her memory. Dare say it'll come back —'

Faro was saved further comment by the sonorous pounding of the dinner gong as the guests took their seats at the table set for fourteen. Only thirteen places were taken, but this fateful number passed without comment as the butler discreetly removed the extra place setting.

If any of the diners noticed the absence of Sir Hedley's niece, they politely ignored it as Elspeth Stuart Millar returned and reinstated her claim upon Inspector Faro. In reply to his question about the young lady's condition, he was told she was recovering nicely. Then Elspeth turned to more important matters, relentlessly pursuing possible scandals in the Royal Family on which Faro, even if he knew they were true, was unable to comment.

Across the table he watched Vince return and, with a nod in his direction, scramble in an undignified manner for a seat as far as possible from the Mad Bart.

The dinner party proceeded without further incident. All excellent courses were consumed, all excellent wines demolished. At last it was time for Detective Inspector Faro to give his talk — so eagerly awaited, according to Terence Lethie's introduction.

His audience knew little of police matters, and in deference to the ladies present, he considered that burglaries were a more appropriate topic for an after-dinner speech than the more bloody and gruesome murders he had solved.

He kept his speech short, aware of the soporific effects that good wining and dining were having on the assembly. Ten minutes later, he sat down to a wave of applause.

'Bravo, bravo,' cried Elspeth at his side. And when the applause had subsided, she said wistfully, 'Perhaps you would care to talk to some of my poor unfortunates — the Society for Impoverished Gentlewomen. I know how greatly they would appreciate —'

Faro was saved an answer as Sara invited the ladies to withdraw and leave the gentlemen to their port and cigars. He was looking forward to that part of the evening, a pleasant relaxation. But it was not to be his.

The butler appeared at Vince's side. A whispered word and he was escorted from the room.

Faro watched them leave, followed by Sir Hedley. Guessing that his stepson had been called to attend the young woman upstairs, he was not kept long in doubt as the butler approached.

'Dr Laurie wishes a word with you, sir.'

Excusing himself and leaving Elspeth mid-sentence, he was escorted into an upstairs bedroom where the Lethies, Vince and Sir Hedley hovered anxiously over Miss Marsh.

Reclining on a sofa, she had been removed from her gown and was now enveloped in a lacy peignoir, presumably the property of her hostess.

Her eyes flickered open. 'It all comes back —' she whispered, and looking around the room, she struggled to sit up.

'Good thing too,' said Sir Hedley, eyeing the ancient ballgown that had been discarded on the bed. 'Mamma's gown from the Queen's Coronation — all I could find. Family heirloom and all that.'

'So this was the unfortunate lady caught in a landslide at Samson's Ribs,' said Faro.

'She was hit by a flying stone, knocked unconscious. Recovered, y'know, staggered along the road. Saw my door —'

'Your mistress,' demanded Terence anxiously. 'When is Her Highness arriving?'

Her Highness?

Faro looked across at Vince, remembering his stepson's fury at being called in to the home of his old enemy. And now it seemed that the injured woman had some connection with the Grand Duchess of Luxoria.

'Your mistress,' Terence repeated patiently. 'Where is she?'

Miss Marsh cried out and looked ready to swoon again.

Sir Hedley stared down at her. 'What are you on about, Lethie?' he said angrily. 'Scared the young miss out of her wits. Don't understand —'

Terence held up his hand. 'Listen to me. This young woman is the Grand Duchess's lady-in-waiting.'

'And her name is Miss Roma Fortescue, Sir Hedley,' said Sara, eyeing him reproachfully.

Miss Fortescue opened her eyes and struggled into a sitting position. 'I remember it all now,' she said weakly.

'Take your time, my dear, tell us what has happened?' said Sara, gently stroking her hands.

'We are as you know on our way to Holyroodhouse. Her Highness was to meet her godmother there —'

Faro listening, frowned. Strange that there had been no mention of this impending visit at the Central Office, where the Queen's movements were followed diligently, especially when she happened to be heading towards Edinburgh. Extra security was a nightmare even on private visits and, as far as the records were concerned, Her Majesty was at this moment still in Balmoral Castle.

'. . . It was the night of the storm, I don't know when —'

'More than a week ago,' put in Terence. 'We had a lot of damage, trees down on the estate.'

'Well, we were delayed. We landed down the coast — somewhere — North Berwick, I think —'

'Are you sure?' asked Faro.

'Yes.'

Faro's frown deepened. What on earth was the

entourage from Luxoria doing landing at North Berwick when Leith was the obvious port?

'. . . The coachman took the wrong route and the road was flooded, a bridge — somewhere — collapsed and we were trying to find a road round when we were swept into the river. I don't remember what happened exactly.'

She shook her head. 'I came to myself lying in a haycart. A carter had fished me out. He told me what had happened, that he was heading to Edinburgh. I felt very uneasy about his attitude, he was —' she paused unhappily '— somewhat over-familiar.'

Even in borrowed robes and a tearful, distressed condition, she still managed to look remarkably attractive, enough for Faro not to find the carter's amorous arousal in the least surprising.

'. . . So I pointed to a house and said that was my destination and the people were expecting me. They would be so glad I was safe —'

Again she paused, biting her lip, reliving that frightening moment. 'It was that village down the road with a church and a loch — we passed on our way here.'

'Duddingston,' prompted Sir Hedley.

She nodded eagerly. 'I was terribly afraid. I waited until the carter was out of sight, then I wandered along the road. I knocked at your door —' She paused and looked at Sir Hedley. 'Then I'm afraid I must have fainted.'

'Quite so, quite so.' Sir Hedley patted her hand and looked up at Vince. 'You know the rest, young fellow. Took her in, saw you passing —'

Faro glanced in Vince's direction. This was not exactly the same story that Vince had told him about a flying stone. Perhaps that had been Miss Fortescue's polite invention to save the embarrassment of that tale of an amorous carter, and Sir Hedley had presumed the rest. He listened intently as she continued:

'Sir Hedley has been so kind to me.' She smiled up at him gratefully. 'He was too much of a gentleman to ask any questions. I thought my memory would never come back — and indeed, until this minute — everyone will be so relieved to know I am unhurt.'

As she spoke, looks were exchanged, looks of growing horror.

Terence bent over her. 'My dear Miss Fortescue, I'm afraid we haven't yet had a sight of Her Highness.'

'You haven't?' She looked round. 'Undoubtedly she will have made her way direct to Holyroodhouse to see Her Majesty.' She smiled for the first time. 'Her Highness is very resourceful. And independent.'

All now looked hopefully towards Faro. He shook his head.

'We have not been informed —'

'But she could be there?' said Miss Fortescue desperately.

'Not without the knowledge of the Edinburgh City Police, miss. You will appreciate that Her Majesty's residences are very carefully guarded —'

'We expected her to arrive at Lethie several days ago,' Terence interrupted. 'When she did not appear, we presumed that she had been delayed. Or that the visit had been cancelled.'

'Tell me, miss, what does your mistress look like?' Faro asked as gently as he could, hoping Miss Fortescue would not realize the sinister implications of such a remark. If she did not, then others did. The reproachful looks in his direction said louder than words that this was a brutal question expressing their own secret and unspoken fears.

Miss Fortescue seemed merely bewildered. She shook her head. 'What does she look like?' she repeated. 'I have a photograph of her. At least — I had one in my luggage. But why — ?' Then as the significance dawned, she whispered: 'You surely don't think —'

'No, no, miss,' Faro lied. 'But if you can tell us a little more about your mistress it would help —'

He quailed under Miss Fortescue's cold stare.

'What is it you wish to know, sir?'

Faro attempted to smile reassuringly, and tried hard not to sound like a grim detective soullessly pursuing information for a missing persons enquiry. He had no alternative but to plunge ahead.

'Her appearance, miss, what she was wearing and so forth.'

Miss Fortescue continued to stare at him, and he carried on hastily, 'Look, miss, presumably your mistress was badly shaken by the accident, as you were. She might have had a shock, the same reactions as you've suffered.' Even as he spoke he felt the possibility of two lost memories was very thin indeed.

Miss Fortescue was clearly having a struggle with her own memory. At last she said: 'She's about my height, a bit more well-built, fairish hair, blue eyes. Does that help?'

It did. That slight description thoroughly alarmed Faro, fitting so neatly the corpse of the woman in the West Bow who had been found in such mysterious circumstances . . . ten days ago.

'The coachman,' said Miss Fortescue helpfully. 'He should be able to tell you what happened. Where he took her and so forth.'

The silence that greeted this observation needed no further explanation. With admirable self-control she stifled a scream.

'You mean — he never — Oh dear — the poor man. He must have drowned.'

Now the same thought was in everyone's mind. Miss Fortescue had indeed been lucky to survive. The coachman and the carriage, and Her Highness the Grand Duchess of Luxoria had not been so fortunate. At this moment, they were lost without trace, swept out by the tide, out of the estuary and into the deep and secret waters of the wild North Sea. They might be washed up anywhere, even in Norway, if their bodies lasted that long.

Faro shuddered. How was this news to be broken to Her Majesty? And to whom would fall the unlucky duty of harbinger of these ill tidings? At least he had no doubt of that man's identity.

Himself.

Taking Sir Terence aside, he explained that he must return to Edinburgh immediately and set some enquiries in motion. He refrained from adding what was surely uppermost in all their minds. A missing Royal duchess who was also the beloved god-daughter of the Queen and the late Prince Consort.

Terence Lethie's heavy sigh indicated that he knew exactly what was at stake. 'Our carriage is at your disposal, sir.'

Faro glanced towards Miss Fortescue. 'A photograph — or a picture — it would help considerably, sir —'

'I'm not sure that we have one.' He nodded towards the anxious group still surrounding Miss Fortescue. 'She will no doubt be able to describe her mistress — a little later, perhaps, when the shock wears off and she is more composed.'

Vince followed him to the door: 'Perhaps I should stay, Stepfather.'

'I think that would be an excellent idea, lad.'

Faro left with some regret. He had been looking forward to a little hard-earned and agreeable relaxation. He would miss tomorrow's tour of the gardens, a chance to see the Crusader's Tomb in the ruined priory and more important, as he was later to discover, the Luck of Lethie.

As he prepared to depart he had an ominous

feeling of disaster, that too much valuable time had already been lost. Twenty-four hours was difficult enough, but ten days . . .

If only Miss Fortescue's unfortunate amnesia had cleared up a little earlier.

As the carriage drove towards Edinburgh, he had ample opportunity to brood upon what had happened to the coachman and more crucially the present whereabouts of the Grand Duchess of Luxoria.

Chapter 6

At Sheridan Place, a message from Superintendent McIntosh awaited Faro. He was to proceed to the Central Office immediately. Realizing that it must be important for the Superintendent to interrupt his weekend, Faro found him as he expected in no good mood.

'You're wanted at Holyrood, straightaway. The usual Royal-visit security formula.'

Faro knew a moment's joy. 'I take it that the Grand Duchess of Luxoria has arrived.'

'Who?' McIntosh looked at him blankly. 'I know nothing about any Grand Duchess. Only that the PM wants a word.' And as Faro went to the door, 'Try not to irritate him, Faro. It doesn't do any of us — particularly yourself — any good, you know.'

Of course he would be patient, Faro decided, clinging to the hope that he had once again allowed his imagination to indulge in morbid fancies. But even his optimism began to fade, faced with the long gallery, its inquisitorial length deliberately chosen to intimidate all but the boldest and most determined. At its far end, Mr Gladstone was pacing the carpet, his already thin-lipped mouth a fast disappearing line across a grimly set countenance.

At Faro's approach, he regarded his watch in some irritation. A stickler for punctuality on all occasions, he grumbled:

'You took your time getting here, Faro.'

'I came from the office immediately, sir.' Faro was damned if he'd apologize.

The watch snapped shut. 'You were summoned yesterday, Inspector.'

Faro was at a loss for an appropriate response. 'Yesterday was Saturday, sir. I was absent from Edinburgh. In fact, I have already had to cut short my weekend with friends.'

He could have said a great deal more on that subject but Gladstone's impatient gesture dismissed such inconvenience as of no importance.

'Friends, indeed?' he snorted. 'Her Majesty's wishes come first, you've been on the job long enough to know that, Faro,' he added severely, his tone indicating that if Faro wasn't fully aware of the fact, then he might soon be seeking other employment.

It had the desired effect. Faro bit back an angry response and said calmly, 'Am I to presume that the arrival of the Grand Duchess of Luxoria is imminent?'

The Prime Minister looked startled. 'So you are aware that she is expected?' Suddenly he thumped his fists together. 'She has not yet put in an appearance. Nor has her arrival been signalled. And that is precisely why you have been summoned, Inspector. Her Majesty is about to leave Balmoral to meet her god-daughter — here. So where the devil is she? Answer me that.'

'I would suggest that she is perhaps making a private visit — to friends —'

'Friends, eh?' The Prime Minister nodded sagely. 'From what I have heard of the lady's unfortunate domestic circumstances, there is no doubt a gentleman involved?' His head inclined to one side, he regarded Faro, extremely pleased with himself for this sharp piece of observation.

'We will, of course, conduct the usual enquiries,' Faro said sternly.

'With the utmost discretion, if you please.'

'Naturally, sir. Now if you will excuse me.'

And giving Mr Gladstone no chance of further questioning, Faro beat a hasty retreat.

Back at the Central Office, Faro thought rapidly. The Superintendent was no fool. He would have to be told and sooner rather than later about the distraught Miss Fortescue.

'It appears that her lady-in-waiting has arrived at Lethie Castle,' he ended the account of his interview with the Prime Minister. 'Her mistress was making a visit there en route to Edinburgh.'

'And so — her present whereabouts?'

'They don't know — precisely. But they expect her arrival imminently,' he ended smoothly, rather proud of this piece of invention, but the Superintendent roared like a wounded lion.

'You realize what this means, Faro. We've mislaid a member of the Royal Family. This could be the end of all our careers. We'll be lucky if we don't see the inside of the Tower. Dear God, what will Her Majesty say to this? You'll have to tell her.' His laugh was without mirth. 'And I don't envy you that.'

'There could be a quite innocent explanation.'

'Could there indeed?'

'The Prime Minister hinted at a secret assignation of a romantic nature.'

'Ah!' McIntosh sighed profoundly. 'Rumour has it that the marriage is fairly unsound. Presumably she has found consolation elsewhere. The PM would of course know about that from information within Royal circles.'

Faro wondered why it had not occurred to the Superintendent as in any way unusual for a Duchess to travel alone. Surely a major concern in the appointment of a lady-in-waiting would be her ability to ignore Royal peccadilloes when necessary.

'. . . But we should have been informed of any change of plan,' the Superintendent continued. 'That is quite unforgivable. After all, our discretion can be relied upon. Who do these foreigners think they are, anyway, keeping Her Majesty waiting?' he added, ignoring the fact that, as he had pointed out, the Grand Duchess was a relative.

'Here —' Turning to the desk he seized a fistful of papers which he flourished under Faro's nose. 'You'd better find her. That's your job.' And as he was leaving: 'I take it that you have some ideas of where to start?'

Faro had a few but none that he would care to discuss with his superior at that moment.

'I think we should play for time, Faro. Presume that Her Highness is, er, on a clandestine visit . . . The message sent ahead could have gone astray. What do you think?'

Faro stifled a smile. The Superintendent could occasionally display an endearingly romantic turn of mind. He was searching for a suitable reply when McIntosh sighed wearily, indicating the interview was at an end.

'Your responsibility, Faro. Be it on your head.'

And Faro didn't care a great deal for the significance of that parting shot either. A chill wind sharp as an axeblade touched the back of his neck as he crossed the corridor into his office, where he earnestly considered the contents of a highly secret file marked 'Her Majesty the Queen'.

Under Luxoria, there was mention of a proposed visit, but no final date had been decided. It simply said that the Grand Duchess would arrive by ship at the port of Leith. Travelling incognito — as befitted a private visit — under the name of Lady Moy, she would be accompanied by her lady-in-waiting, Miss Roma Fortescue. There was no mention of any coachman or equerry travelling with them.

Faro's dismal thoughts were interrupted by Constable Reid.

'There's a lady come to see you. She's in the waiting room.'

'Show her in.' Faro's immediate hope was that this was Miss Fortescue bearing a photograph of her mistress, and he was somewhat taken aback to find that his visitor was Lady Lethie.

As they shook hands he said: 'I'm glad to see you here, I was about to come out to Aberlethie. How is Miss Fortescue?'

'Much improved.' She smiled. 'We have persuaded her to accept our hospitality until — until things sort themselves out. She will be more comfortable with us, and now that her memory has returned she does not feel she can impose any further on Sir Hedley. Although, of course, his place is more adjacent to Holyrood.'

Her frown indicated that the decision had been difficult. Faro thought that it was all too obvious to anyone who had ever set foot — or nose — within the walls of Solomon's Tower.

As she spoke she opened her reticule, but instead of the photograph Faro now hoped was the reason for her visit, she took out a dainty lace handkerchief and patted her nose.

'Fortunately, I can provide her with items from my wardrobe, we are of the same size — until her luggage arrives — eventually,' she added, but Faro felt there was little hope in the word or in her expression as she said it.

'Miss Fortescue still has no idea of what might have happened to her mistress?'

'Not the slightest. We do try to keep her spirits

up, Inspector, we try to get her to look on the bright side. But it is extremely hard, very hard indeed. She is prone to the most gloomy thoughts.' She paused before adding:

'She could, of course, have gone to Holyrood. I think that was in her mind at one point. But as you see, that would not do at all. She is most anxious that there is no fuss, as she calls it. The Grand Duchess would be most distressed when she, er, arrives.'

'But, surely — look, Lady Lethie, I have it on good authority that the Queen is on her way down from Balmoral. Once she arrives, then Miss Fortescue must go and tell her what has happened.'

'Oh, so Her Majesty is coming.' Sara Lethie smiled. She looked oddly relieved by this information. 'Perhaps you will let us know immediately she arrives. I do hope it will be very soon as we are due to go to France for a family wedding —'

And Sara Lethie stood up and drew on her gloves. Conscious of her air of relief, he decided to spare her the painful details of his interview with the Prime Minister.

'I do hope you will forgive me intruding upon you in this way, Inspector. I'm sure you are a very busy man, but as I was coming to Edinburgh today — one of my committees, you know — I decided I must try and see if there was any further news I could take to Miss Fortescue.' She paused for breath.

'She really is most anxious. In fact, we all are. Everyone is pretending that there will be a perfectly logical reason for the Grand Duchess not arriving, but after the accident —' She shuddered.

'How well did you know Miss Fortescue?'

Sara Lethie looked startled by the question, but only for a moment. She managed a nervous laugh. 'Not at all really. But the Fortescues have been friends of ours for — oh, generations. Roma's father is a court official in Luxoria. They have served the Grand Duchy since the eighteenth century when they followed Prince Charles Edward Stuart's father into exile.'

She looked at him earnestly. 'You will keep us informed, Inspector — when you have any further news.'

'Immediately, Lady Lethie.'

At the door she turned. 'Do you think this could be the work of, well, some foreign conspiracy?'

'That thought had not occurred to me.' So she wasn't aware of the unsound marriage and the possibility of a romantic assignation. 'Are you suggesting that the Grand Duchess might have been kidnapped?'

If only that were true, he thought. That she was still alive, and in one piece.

'Something like that, perhaps.'

'I'm sure you're mistaken, Lady Lethie. However, it would be a great help if you had a photograph of Her Highness — solely for our purposes. You can rely on our discretion.'

Sara Lethie frowned. 'I think there might be one, taken a long time ago. Possibly Miss Fortescue will have one of a more recent date.' She smiled. 'I'm sure she'll be best able to help you. They have been together since childhood. Very close, you know, grew up together. Why don't you talk to her?'

That was precisely what Faro intended. A personal talk with the lady-in-waiting would better suit the purpose of his enquiries than any picture of the missing woman. His growing misgivings weren't helped by Constable Reid handing him a reply to his telegraph to the North Berwick constabulary:

'No wreckage of coach on road or shore reported.'

As he was leaving, the Superintendent caught him at the door. 'Message from Balmoral, Faro. Her Majesty has had a slight chill and is to remain indoors for a day or two on the advice of her physicians. Let's hope her god-daughter deigns to appear before the Queen arrives. If not, heads will roll,' he added grimly.

Faro shuddered as he closed the door.

He had not seen Vince since his return from Lethie Castle when he had been called away on an urgent and difficult confinement.

'All is well,' he said as they met at supper that night. 'Mother and son doing famously.'

'How did you leave your patient at Aberlethie?'

'Miss Fortescue? Seemed to be making a fine

72

recovery. Healthy young woman, despite a tendency to the vapours. Any further developments in the saga of her missing mistress?'

For Vince's benefit, Faro went over the details of his interview with Mr Gladstone and of Lady Lethie's visit.

Vince frowned. 'I think the romantic assignation is a bit thin, Stepfather. Surely Miss Fortescue would know if she and the Duchess are such close companions?' He paused then added: 'What do you think of the kidnapping idea?'

'We must consider it as a possibility. But bearing in mind the complexity of Luxorian politics and that the Duchess was forced into a loveless marriage, the odious President might have good reason to want rid of her. But, I suspect, on a more permanent basis than mere kidnapping,' he added grimly.

'A closer acquaintance with Miss Fortescue might indeed bring forth some illuminating thoughts on that subject,' said Vince.

Faro smiled. 'Would you care to volunteer?'

'Alas, no. She isn't quite my type, Stepfather. Pretty and all that, but there's — well, something strange about her. Too reserved — and foreign for me, despite all that good solid British education. She wasn't much in evidence over the weekend and the Mad Bart took himself off, grateful, I think, that the Lethies were willing to look after her. We managed a few rounds of golf and a look at the Luck o' Lethie.'

'Stuart Millar told me it was worth seeing.'

Vince shrugged. 'It's just a battered old horn that hangs in a glass case in the old chapel, the only part of the castle they didn't pull down, in fact. Apparently it was brought back from King Solomon's Temple by the crusader David de Lethie — the one whose tomb is in the priory.'

'Why is it called the Luck o' Lethie?'

Vince smiled. 'Legend has it that as long as it survives, so will the Lethie line continue. Considering the swarm of offspring, and the deafening noise they were making, there seems little doubt about it.' He sighed. 'But none of this helps much with our missing Grand Duchess, does it?'

Faro looked at him. 'Vince, I've had a terrible thought.'

'You're too ready to look on the gloomy side, Stepfather. It's one of your failings. You know that. You must try to keep it under control,' he added severely, and at Faro's expression, he continued, 'Look, the fact that she's still missing doesn't necessarily mean that she's been drowned — or kidnapped, Stepfather. It could be something quite innocuous, as has been suggested, a visit to a secret lover. After all, this is no ordinary missing person —'

Vince stopped suddenly. The same thought was in both of their minds. A woman's body, unidentified, that didn't fit any description on the missing persons list at the Central Office.

'Dear God,' Vince whispered. 'You're surely not thinking — there could be some connection between the — West Bow corpse —'

Faro looked at him slowly and Vince jumped to his feet.

'Oh, no — she couldn't be — could she?' he added weakly.

When Faro didn't reply, Vince sat down again sharply. As sickening realization dawned they regarded each other with mounting horror across the table, neither fully able to complete the dreadful thought.

That, even as they spoke, Dr Cranley's medical students might be deeply absorbed in dissecting what remained of Amelie, Duchess of Luxoria, the well-beloved god-daughter of Her Majesty the Queen.

Chapter 7

Faro slept little that night.

His thoughts like rats trapped in a cage, he searched in vain for the vital clue that he was certain he had overlooked or whose significance he had failed to recognize when it had been presented to him. Such shortcomings, damnable in his profession, were by no means a novel experience, but left always the dry sensation of defeat in his mouth, the dreaded whisper: was he losing his skill?

He took a deep breath. There was only one solution: before visiting Aberlethie again, and talking to Miss Fortescue, he must return to the discovery of the woman's body in the West Bow and prove to himself — somehow — that his suspicions regarding her identity were false.

After a hasty breakfast without Vince, who had been summoned to attend a sick patient, Faro set off for the Central Office by the short cut through Gibbet Lane, bordering Solomon's Tower.

On an impulse he decided to call upon Sir Hedley. Eight o'clock was striking on the city clocks as he approached the door, but he had no doubt that the old man would be up and about. It was Sir Hedley's proud boast that he rose with

76

the larks and retired with the setting sun.

The tower was gloomy and forbidding in darkness, and much the same even in the daylight of a grey Edinburgh morning, which did little to raise Faro's spirits as he applied his hand to the rusted and ancient bell-pull. The clanging sound reverberated heartily through the surrounding area but failed to bring any response.

Deciding that Sir Hedley must be deaf indeed not to have been roused by the din, he observed with some unease that the front door was very slightly ajar. It yielded instantly to his touch. Was this no more than a nocturnal convenience for the cats, he wondered as they assailed him from all directions with yowls of protest that he had not arrived carrying saucers of milk? Only the boldest, however, were confident enough to sidle out and insinuate themselves around his ankles.

'Sir Hedley! Sir Hedley!'

There was no reply and Faro decided that he was getting unduly nervous. There was absolutely no reason why Sir Hedley should not be away from home, he might have visited friends and stayed the night. An unduly optimistic thought, Faro decided, knowing the nature of the reclusive occupant's character.

With a growing sense of foreboding, he carefully pushed his way inside, as cats of every colour, shape and age noisily scampered after his ankles, anxious not to let this possible source of sustenance out of their sight.

'Sir Hedley? Sir Hedley?'

Silence greeted him. Opening the door, he stepped carefully into the stone-walled parlour, and averting his eyes to its squalor and his nose to its odours, he tried not to breathe too deeply as he climbed the twisting staircase to the upper floor. Dreading what he might find inside, he opened an ancient studded door. A bedroom, at first glance no better than the apartment he had just left.

His inclination was to close the door again hastily. Instead he approached the bed. Half a dozen privileged cats gave him haughty stares from the comfort of a plumed four-poster. Faro suspected that it dated back to the seventeenth century when necessity dictated that grand beds were built into upper rooms approached by a turnpike stair. Since there was no method of transporting them either up or down afterwards, many thus survived both the attentions of thieving enemies and the changing fashions of time.

Faro approached the bed cautiously. Sir Hedley wasn't lying there with his throat cut as imagination had so readily prompted, but his cats were very much at home, resting on the remains of a once well-made and handsome garment, certainly not the property of Sir Hedley. The delicate lace and embroidered bodice, stained by cats and ripped by their claws, suggested that this was yet another of the Dowager Lady Marsh's elegant cast-offs.

The sight offended Faro, deeply. By no means a frugal man, he deplored such waste. Such a gown, now a bed for cats, would have fetched an excellent price in Edinburgh's luckenbooths, and provided meals in plenty for many a starving family.

Without any further compunction about searching the house for the missing baronet, he went down a few steps and opened an old studded door, where there was another surprise in store.

He was in a stone-walled chapel-like apartment. Instead of the religious symbols its mitred roof suggested, here were the accoutrements of the Ancient Order of Templars. Doubtless Sir Hedley had belonged to the order in his youth, as did so many of the nobility. But what struck Faro as extraordinary was that the room was clean and obviously well-tended and completely out of character with the sordid condition of the rest of the house. Who then was the guardian of this shrine, for Sir Hedley seemed an improbable choice?

The sight of this serene chapel left him with a sense of disquiet, as he pondered other inconsistencies such as Sir Hedley's apparently innocent role as rescuer of Miss Fortescue.

Had he misjudged Sir Hedley, dismissed him as a harmless eccentric? Was Vince's loathing unconsciously justified and did the Mad Bart, in fact, hold a sinister role in the Grand Duchess's disappearance?

By the time he had put some distance between himself and Solomon's Tower, the thought of Sir Hedley's complicity became even more unlikely, and as he approached the High Street, his sense of logic reasserted itself.

The truth was undoubtedly that he had been too involved with his own distaste for the West Bow. His eagerness to get the investigation over with as soon as possible had permitted the unforgivable in a detective. He had allowed his preoccupation with bitter personal emotions regarding his long-dead father to blunt his normally acute powers of observation and deduction.

With a dawning sense of horror at a nightmare that had already begun and from which there was no probable awakening, he could no longer delay reliving the scene from that moment Constable Reid summoned him from his carriage to view a beggar-woman's corpse.

This time he would proceed as a diligent detective on the look-out for anything even slightly out of the ordinary that would never be considered except in a possible murder investigation.

He stepped into the Central Office to be hailed by Danny McQuinn, who had newly returned from Aberdeen. Faro was glad to see his young sergeant again and after a few moments' social conversation, he decided that McQuinn had better become acquainted with the case of the missing Grand Duchess. Once the bane of his life, the passing years had smoothed the rough edges of the Irishman's personality. Trust, respect and even grudging admiration had grown between the two men.

In addition, Faro recognized with gratitude that, on more than one occasion, he owed his life to McQuinn's quick thinking. And this had extended to members of Faro's family.

McQuinn was sharp, none better, and Faro was consoled that he made no immediate connection between the missing Duchess and the dead vagrant in the West Bow. Or at least if he did, then he refrained from comment.

'Drownings in the Forth, sir? Nothing reported. Weather's been good since the storm,' McQuinn added.

'Try further afield, McQuinn. Bodies can be carried right across the estuary to the coast of Fife or down the East Lothian coast.'

'What sort of a corpse are we looking for, sir?'

'A coachman, possibly in some sort of livery.'

'I take it he was driving the lady's carriage.'

'Yes.'

McQuinn thought for a moment. 'As both are missing, could there be some connection? I mean, like kidnapping, holding her to ransom.'

'I've thought of that.'

'The newspaper might have a photograph of her, sir. I dare say this Miss Fortescue will oblige with a description of the coachman. Servants usually know one another uncommonly well.'

Faro watched as McQuinn pocketed his notebook, thankful that he could be relied on.

'I'll check with the North Berwick harbour authorities. With luck I might find someone who knew — or saw — this coachman. Shall I go to Aberlethie, talk to Miss Fortescue?'

'No. Leave that to me,' said Faro.

But first, the Wizard's House.

Faro's route to the West Bow took him close by the Grassmarket, a part of Edinburgh which had witnessed many grisly executions in Scotland's history. And here, he thought, he stood on the threshold of what might prove to be yet another sensational case in the annals of that country's crime.

But as his footsteps led him through the Lawnmarket past his cousin's lodging, he was guiltily aware that he was sorely neglecting Leslie Faro Godwin. The temptation to do something normal again, to see a pleasant smiling face, to talk to a man whose only interest in crime was its value as a news item, was overwhelming.

As Faro walked along the narrow Wynd his nostrils were assailed by increasingly unpleasant odours of cooking, cats and human excrement.

Looking up at the bleak lodging, once more his mind flew in vivid contrast to his own comfortable but mainly empty house in Sheridan Place. Doubtless it would be useless to try and persuade his cousin to change his mind. Too much time had been lost, the indication had been that Leslie Faro Godwin intended his stay in Edinburgh to be brief.

Faro smiled wryly. What would his mother make of all this? It was some time since he had written to her in Orkney and his conscience smote him regularly on his neglect of his daughters, Rose and Emily, who were fortunate indeed to receive even a postcard from him on rare occasions.

He could almost hear his mother's reproachful sigh when she heard about Leslie Faro Godwin. A firm believer in: 'There's no one like your own flesh and blood', she would be horrified at his treatment of a close relative, despite any reminders that the Godwins had abandoned her after her husband was killed. 'That was a long time ago,' she would say, 'you've both come a long way since then. Thank God.'

There was no response to his rap on the front door. It was unlocked and he entered a dank dim corridor where doors on either side indicated other apartments. Following a narrow, evil-smelling stair twisting upwards, he found himself outside the first-floor apartment which Leslie had indicated from the street. Here was a more promising door, and Faro tapped on it. As he awaited a response, he heard voices within. His cousin was at home.

The door was opened by a tall, dark and swarthy man of villainous aspect. A pock-marked countenance was not helped by a huge scar which puckered one side of his face. He looked like an old soldier who had seen many campaigns, and even as Faro awaited his reply as to whether his cousin Mr Leslie Faro Godwin was at home, he decided that, used as he was to dealing with violent men, this one belonged in the category he would have avoided encountering on a dark night.

'Someone to see you, maister.' Faro recognized the voice as one of the two he had heard.

'Who is it, Batey?'

So this was Sergeant Batey. A man with the cold dead eyes of a killer. No doubt he was loyal to his master. Certainly, Leslie Godwin would be safe wherever he went with this man to look after him.

'Sez he's yer cousin.'

'Jeremy? Do come in —'

Godwin was alone, seated near the window. He rose to greet Faro, book in hand. The window was tiny, and the dim light revealed a room furnished with only the meagre essentials. There were two other doors, which might lead either into more rooms or into cupboards.

Godwin's greeting was cheerful. He cut short Faro's apologies.

'No need for that, Jeremy. I'm always full of good intentions and promises that I never manage to fulfil. With the best will in the world, time just runs away with me.'

He paused, giving Faro a curious look. 'Any developments with your West Bow vagrant?' he asked eagerly.

Faro hesitated then shook his head, anxious that the fewer who knew about the missing woman, the better for all concerned. Particularly himself. So he decided against mentioning Miss Fortescue, realizing that however loyal a cousin, the newsman who was also Godwin might find the temptation of pursuing such a story irresistible, thereby making it public property with results that would be nothing short of disastrous.

Leslie had observed his hesitation, for he smiled. 'I scent a story somewhere.'

'I'm afraid we didn't get very far with our enquiries.'

'I've seen that lad who found her a few times, by the way. Sandy, wasn't that his name? Batey caught him with his hand in my pocket the other day. He lives just round the corner in one of the tall lands, Bowheads Wynd, they call it.'

This was an unexpected stroke of luck. 'There are a few questions I'd like to ask him about that night.'

Godwin looked at him. 'D'you know, I had the same feeling. That he knew a lot more than he was telling us. For instance, I shouldn't be at all surprised if he knew what happened to the woman's clothes.'

'Clothes?' Faro was a little taken aback by this astute observation.

Godwin laughed. 'Surely, Jeremy, you saw at once that the dead woman was no vagrant. Such hair and hands never went with a beggar's gown. They belonged with silks and satins, with jewels and fine clothes.'

'So you think they might have been removed?'

Leslie nodded eagerly. 'Undoubtedly the case.

And the lad Sandy might have been scared to rob a corpse himself but he would have soon seen the possibilities of making some profit out of those who don't share such a sense of delicacy. It was probably all taken care of, long before he was sent to summon the police.'

'You could be right,' said Faro.

'Of course I'm right.' Leslie continued: 'From my slight acquaintance with the Grassmarket, I see plenty of booths selling clothes for pennies. Mostly rags.'

Pausing, he studied Faro thoughtfully. 'But what we might dismiss as rags would keep a poor family in food for a week.'

Faro smiled wryly. Obviously he wasn't the only member of his family who had inherited the ability to observe and deduce.

'A splendid idea, Leslie. Well worth following. But not what I came for — Shall we have dinner one night? Say, the Café Royale? Saturday evening at seven?'

Accompanying him to the door, Godwin said: 'Look, I'd like to help. Seeing that I was in at the very beginning, there with you, so to speak, when the woman was found. If I see the lad Sandy again, I'll try and buy some information for you. A few pence might work wonders at loosening his tongue. Really — I mean it.'

He put a hand on Faro's arm. 'I want to help you solve your beggar-woman mystery. Not only for the news value either.' He grinned. 'Just because I enjoy a challenge.'

Faro left him and walked down the stone stairs, suddenly happy and confident. Having his cousin's assistance was exactly what he needed to solve this baffling case.

Chapter 8

Faro's route to the West Bow took him past the entrance to Bowheads Wynd, where he decided to call on young Sandy. A couple of shillings thrust into his hand, with the promise of more to come, should be ample to loosen the lad's tongue about his gruesome discovery and the events which took place before he summoned Constable Reid to the scene.

Faro had to knock on several doors before he received even a scowling oath in response to his enquiry. Whereas his cousin's lodging was merely shabby and poor, Bowheads Wynd was depressingly lacking in hope as well as cleanliness of any kind.

From each opened door, his nose was overwhelmed by the stench of crowded humanity within. He remembered that these tall 'lands' had once been the pride of Edinburgh, town residences to the nobility, lived in by one family only — along with their many servants. Now each room on all six floors was occupied by perhaps twelve people — a man and woman, their swarm of children and maybe a couple of elderly relatives or hangers-on.

He had almost given up hope of finding Sandy when at last a woman, with several small children clinging to her skirts, answered to the name of Mrs Dunnock. Her clothes were clean, shabby but neat, and when she spoke she nervously pushed a gold bracelet back from her wrist.

'I'm his ma. What d'ye want wi' him? What's he done this time?' she said wearily, her manner that of a parent used to receiving constant complaints about her unruly offspring.

'Nothing. Just tell him Inspector Faro came by.'

'Inspector Faro?'

Mention of his name panicked her. She stepped backwards, glancing over her shoulder as if someone else might be listening.

'You're a polis!' she said accusingly, as if he had wheedled his way to her door under false pretences.

'I'm a detective, Mrs Dunnock.'

She took a great gulp of air, her hands clutched at her wrists and she pointed to his tweed cape and hat. 'Proper polismen wear uniforms.'

'Detectives don't.'

'And that gives you the right to come poking your nose into what don't concern you. We ain't done nothing wrong,' she added in a pathetic whine.

'Neither has Sandy — at least not that we know about,' he said. 'Just tell him that there's a couple of shillings for him to put to good use.'

The woman's eyes glittered at the mention of money, almost as if he had given her a glimpse into paradise. Her defensive manner softened so rapidly, he guessed that this was obviously not what she had been fearing as the outcome of his unexpected visit.

She managed a smile. 'He's no' at home, but I'll tell him, mister. Where d'ye bide?'

'He knows that too,' said Faro, and lifted his hat politely as he walked away down the steps.

An adept at shallow breathing, he was glad to fully extend his lungs again, for even the reek of smoking chimneys in the High Street was ambrosia compared to the vile stench in the fetid house he had just left, with its dreadful odour of rotting meat. God only knew what cheap cuts the poor got from the flesher's disease-ridden stocks, and why many more did not succumb to food poisoning. And as always his final thought when faced with direst poverty was: But for the grace of God, there go I. For such he was fully aware might have been the squalid circumstances of his own life, but for an accident of fate that had made him a policeman's son with a widowed mother prepared to make material sacrifices for his education.

Even in broad daylight, with a thin sun turning the Castle into the setting for one of Sir Walter Scott's romances, Faro approached the wizard Major's abode with reluctance. Its chilling atmosphere and sinister emanations had remained untouched by passing years and changing seasons. Facing north-east its windows were untroubled by sunshine, but it was not aspect alone which added to the feeling of foreboding and melancholy.

Clocks from all over the city were striking eleven o'clock, and it was a bright sunny autumn morning, yet Faro observed how passersby avoided the tall shadow thrown across the narrow cobbled street by the Wizard's House. Men hurried along, heads down, while women, wrapping shawls closer about their heads, drew small children more closely to their sides with a hushed word of warning.

Through the doorway with its ironic inscription, '*Soli deo honor et gloria*, 1604', Faro proceeded along the low vaulted passage which led through the tall land to a narrow court behind. There, solitary and sinister, stood the entrance to Major Weir's house. Legend had it that the wizard had cast a spell on the neighbouring turnpike stair so that anyone climbing up it felt as if they were instead climbing down — to the infernal regions below being no doubt the implication.

Faro shuddered. Only the appalling coincidence of a woman's body and a missing duchess, the nightmare possibility that they might be connected, had driven him back to this hell house.

His last visit had been made in darkness, now every detail of the building, every stone might conceal a vital clue to the mystery. He felt suddenly hopeful. The discovery of a corpse pronounced as 'dead from natural causes' would involve no search for clues except for the purpose of identification.

The door was slightly ajar. Hanging by one

creaking hinge, it was unlocked and Faro doubted whether it had seen a key for that purpose in living memory. With only the vaguest idea of what he was looking for, what might be of significance in this puzzling case, Faro was suddenly hopeful. Long undisturbed dust is of admirable assistance to a man searching for evidence of violence and the Major's house was most obliging in this respect. In the thick coating on the floor were the recent footprints of the policemen intermingled with tiny animal tracks identifiable as rats and mice.

Closer observation revealed a clean but wide trail in the centre of the dirt from the front door into the squalid scene of death, ending at the place where the body had been found. He sat back on his heels. Some of the dust had caked into mud. He crumbled it in his hands. Something, or more likely, someone had been dragged along the floor, someone whose garments were wet. Searching carefully again he discovered threads, a piece of cloth caught on a rusty nail. No ordinary cloth either but a shred of fine lace, which he pocketed carefully.

A little further into the room, near an inside drain, the light from the dim window above touched a thin line of gold. He bent down and dragged out a chain bearing an ornamental cross.

Not a Christian crucifix but an eight-pointed cross pattée.

Faro sat back on his heels, weighing it in his hand. He wished he hadn't found it here, for he had seen this emblem of the Templars very recently. On a backcloth in the chapel in Solomon's Tower.

And a chill — cold and malevolent as the wizard's ghostly hand — stole over him as he remembered that Major Weir had been a Templar as well as a member of the Edinburgh City Guard.

Did this indicate a further sinister twist to the mystery and did the solution to this nineteenth-century disappearance have its roots back in history?

Taking it a step further, was the Mad Bart's Tower a Temple of Solomon and Sir Hedley Marsh the last of its guardians? Could his life as an eccentric and a recluse be a disguise for a secret and never-ending quest?

No. It was too preposterous a theory even for Faro. Besides, it led him far from the missing Grand Duchess, a mystery which must be solved urgently if he was not to find himself facing an irate Prime Minister.

He had a great deal to think about as he sat on the train to Aberlethie. He enjoyed train journeys. Staring out of the window at the passing countryside gave him leisure to get his facts in order and make a few notes.

A halt had been conveniently arranged with the railway company where the line passed over Lethie estate grounds. The walk to the castle through the little hamlet with its cluster of houses was delightful.

He stopped to watch the horses being led across the fields, gathering in the late harvest with the seagulls screaming at their tracks as the uplifted soil revealed fresh delicacies of worms.

Deciding he was in no hurry after all, Faro lit a pipe and leaned on a fence to watch this pastoral and peaceful scene. Around him lay evidence of all those earlier settlements which had held their sway in Scotland's history, then one by one had disappeared. And in the fullness of time, Faro realized, this must be the fate of his own era, too, giving place to a new world waiting in the wings and a destiny as yet unborn. But all would owe their origins to those centuries long gone which had formed the traditions of the Scotland in which he now stood.

When almost reluctantly he at last walked up the stone steps to the castle he was told that Miss Fortescue was walking with the laird in the gardens.

'They went in the direction of the old priory.'

The neat lawns and geometric flowerbeds surrounding the castle gave way to a wild garden, the domain of ancient trees of huge girth. Through them could be glimpsed a distant sea, glittering on the horizon, and a ruined wall thrusting into the sky.

Here was the twelfth-century Priory of Our Lady which had once dominated the whole area. Its buildings and harbour, once vital links in a flourishing port, had vanished with a retreating coastline that had left an estuary of the River

Forth no longer deep enough to allow sailing ships and steamers safe harbour.

For a little while, Aberlethie had acquired notoriety and the close attention of the exciseman as a landing place for smugglers and those on dubious errands and journeys, with their own reasons for entering Scotland at secret and safe locations.

As he made his way through the dense shrubbery, Faro heard voices which halted him in his tracks. Although the words were indistinct, what he was overhearing was undoubtedly a fierce argument.

Reluctant to make his presence known, he decided on immediate retreat, but his cautious withdrawal from the scene had not taken into account the laird's dogs, who pricked up their ears and barking fiercely darted towards this intruder.

With Sir Terence calling them sharply to heel, Faro emerged somewhat sheepishly, endeavouring to look as cheerful as was possible in the circumstances.

Sir Terence and Miss Fortescue were standing by the Crusader's Tomb in its niche in the one remaining wall of the priory. They were not alone. Another figure emerged. Sir Hedley Marsh.

At the sight of him, Faro's relief that he was very much alive was intermingled with curiosity about what he was doing here, a participant in a conspiratorial conversation.

Miss Fortescue, he noticed, had fully recovered

and looked none the worse for her recent ordeal. In fact, she looked decidedly pretty. As she came towards him, hand outstretched in smiling greeting, she appeared to be in perfect command of the situation.

Obviously Lady Lethie had been generous with her extensive wardrobe, he thought approvingly. The two ladies were of similar height and dimensions. Miss Fortescue, carrying a lace parasol and wearing a muslin afternoon gown covered in tiny sprigs of flowers, provided an attractive picture for any man.

'How nice to see you, Inspector,' she said, and he had an odd feeling that she meant it.

As he exchanged greetings with Sir Hedley, Faro decided to avoid any mention of his morning visit to Solomon's Tower.

'Sir Hedley has been giving us a history lesson on our Crusader,' said Sir Terence.

'I'm sure Mr Faro would like to hear it,' Miss Fortescue added with an anxious glance that begged his interest.

But the looks exchanged between the three suggested that this was by no means all that had been under discussion. And Sir Hedley, with much clearing of throat, stared anxiously in the direction of the Crusader's Tomb, his manner suggesting one hard-pressed for immediate inspiration.

He rose to the task gallantly. 'David de Lethie was one of a band of Scottish knights who survived the Crusades in Jerusalem and returned to fight at the side of his king, Robert the Bruce, at

Bannockburn. There are some discrepancies about this effigy. His sword arm, for instance.'

Faro looked down at the worn stone of the coffin, which had been broken open centuries ago when whatever remained of the Crusader had been removed. As for the once-proud helmeted face lying eyes open to the sky, the harsh elements of East Lothian wind and weather had all but obliterated his noble features.

'The sword arm,' Sir Hedley repeated. 'Crusaders always had their right arm crossing over on to their sword hilt on the left side — so —' He demonstrated. 'De Lethie however, did not.'

Faro looked down on the effigy. 'Rather looks as if he was holding something in his sword arm.'

'But what?' Sir Terence nodded. 'That's a mystery we've been trying to solve for centuries past.'

Sir Hedley turned to Faro. 'What was he holding that was more important than a sword, d'you think?'

'Perhaps you can tell us, Faro,' Sir Terence cut in. 'You're the detective, after all.'

Faro smiled. 'My province is recent deaths not those of six hundred years ago.'

'There must be some clues.' There was a note of desperation in Miss Fortescue's voice which made the three men all look at her quickly, and all for different reasons. Curiosity — and perhaps even warning.

Faro turned his attention to the effigy. 'I'd say what he was carrying was a chalice.' He looked again. 'Or a staff of some kind.'

'A staff?' they repeated.

The sun dipped low and the silence that followed this observation seemed to last for several moments.

'Undoubtedly Inspector Faro is right.' Sir Terence sounded as if the words were being forced out of him. 'I wonder why?' he added lightly.

'More important, what happened to it? Interesting to know that,' said Sir Hedley.

'Interesting, indeed,' said Faro. 'The evidence would suggest that you aren't the first to give this matter serious consideration, sir.'

He pointed to the broken coffin on which the effigy rested. 'It must have taken considerable force to open that and remove the body. And whatever treasures it held.'

The word 'treasure' stunned them again into momentary silence.

'We suspect that it happened in the sixteenth century when the priory was sacked during the Reformation, long before the castle was built,' said Sir Terence at last.

'You think — that whatever — they were looking for — might have been buried with him,' said Miss Fortescue.

'That is the general opinion.'

'Grave robbers rarely leave sworn testimonies of how and why. Is there nothing in the family records, sir?'

Lethie shook his head. 'Nothing earlier than the sixteenth century and very sparse afterwards. Only the main events were considered worthy of posterity, like the brief visit Queen Mary and Bothwell made shortly after their marriage. But the family's enthusiasm didn't extend to her descendant Prince Charles Edward Stuart. Or if it did, then they were too discreet to put it on record.' He looked at Faro. 'So all we have on the Crusader is legend.'

'Was he a Templar by any chance?' Faro asked.

'Perhaps.' The reply was vague. 'It is possible.'

It was more than possible, seeing that the Crusader's shield bore upon it the still decipherable cross pattée. Odd that Sir Hedley failed to recognize the significance of something he encountered daily in his own house.

More worrying still was the possible significance of that same cross found on a broken chain in the Wizard's House in the West Bow, a fact Faro felt was linked with the body whose identity he was increasingly and most unhappily aware might prove to be the Grand Duchess of Luxoria.

'It's all very strange, isn't it?' said Miss Fortescue. Shivering she drew her shawl closer around her shoulders and Sir Terence seized upon the gesture with relief.

'You are cold, m'dear. Let us return to the house. You will come with us, Inspector, take some refreshment.'

As he accompanied them he realized no one had asked him his business there, or why he had suddenly appeared as they were talking by the tomb.

They were much too polite. In fact no one

showed the slightest curiosity about his presence. As if a visit from a Detective Inspector investigating the mysterious non-arrival of the Queen's god-daughter was a commonplace event in their lives.

Surely the first question his appearance should have aroused in that conspiratorial group he had disturbed, was: 'What news of Her Highness?'

Chapter 9

As they walked towards the house, Faro's responses to Sir Terence's remarks about weather, crops and estate management were quite automatic. One of his useful accomplishments was the ability to carry on an agreeable conversation while his mind dealt with more important matters.

The Crusader, David de Lethie, had been a Templar, bearing the cross pattée on his shield. That Sir Hedley Marsh was connected with them, too, was evident from the chapel, so unexpectedly immaculate amid the squalor of Solomon's Tower. And from Vince, Faro knew that Sir Terence was a Templar as well as being a Grand Master in the Freemasons, whose origins and rituals were based on that society. But of perhaps even greater significance, Major Weir, the seventeenth-century owner of the Wizard's House, had also been a Templar. That he had terrified citizens by his identification with the devil and his ability to perform magic tricks, Faro was sure fitted somewhere into a pattern concerning the dead woman's identity and the reason for her death.

Faro sighed, wishing he could interpret above Lethie's polite remarks, the low-pitched murmurings between Sir Hedley and Miss Fortescue. Was there some conspiratorial connection between these three people, some deadly link with the gold cross on its broken chain in Weir's Land?

He was rapidly discarding his original suspicion that a murder had taken place in the West Bow. All the evidence suggested that she had already been dead when she was carried into the Wizard's House.

As he sat politely through the ritual of afternoon tea, served with great elegance by Lady Lethie, his eyes wandered constantly in the direction of Miss Fortescue. She was not only extremely good to look at, he decided, but she also had undeniable presence, the aura of authority that was perhaps the first requirement of a Royal lady-in-waiting.

Sir Hedley Marsh sat at her side and monopolized her completely. While she gave smiling, patient answers to some bumbling nonsense about fishing in Dunsapie Loch, Faro considered what measures he must take to direct this pleasant but ineffectual teatime conversation towards the object of his visit: namely, the promised photograph or picture of Duchess Amelie, now so vital to his search.

The clock melodiously chimed four, reminding him that the train from North Berwick to Edinburgh was due at the Aberlethie halt in less than an hour.

'May I help you to a piece of cake?' said Lady Lethie with an encouraging smile, aware of his empty plate and distracted air.

'No, thank you. I wonder — the photograph?' he reminded her gently.

Although the words were spoken quietly, his question succeeded in bringing all conversation to an abrupt end.

Sara Lethie smiled at him vaguely, shaking her head in the apologetic manner of one who had forgotten entirely: 'Of course. Of course, you wanted a photograph, didn't you.' And to her husband. 'Terence — do we have a picture somewhere?'

Sir Terence responded with alacrity. 'No, my dear. Not in the album, I've already had a glance.' And to Faro: 'I did think we had one taken at Holyrood, but I must have been mistaken.'

'Would have been a long time ago. Mere child. Not much use to you now, I'm afraid,' Sir Hedley put in.

Faro turned to Miss Fortescue. 'What about you, miss? Do you happen to possess a recent photograph of your mistress?'

Miss Fortescue shook her head sadly. 'There was one, very recent — a present for Her Majesty, you know. In a silver frame. But I'm afraid it is beneath the waters of the Forth now, with all the rest of our possessions.'

Faro stood up abruptly. So that was that. His journey to Aberlethie had been a waste of time when he could have been pursuing more urgent and productive enquiries in Edinburgh. But not one of these polite, well-bred people thought that an apology was due for his wasted effort.

'If you will forgive me. My train, you know.'

'Of course, Inspector. Of course. Sorry you

must leave us,' said Sir Terence with undue heartiness. An angry and frustrated Faro felt that was a lie. They were not in the least sorry to see the back of him.

Then as if his urgent thoughts had communicated themselves to Miss Fortescue, she rose to her feet.

'If Inspector Faro is ready to leave now, I will walk with him to the railway halt.'

The Lethies exchanged worried glances. They sprang to their feet, followed a little creakily by Sir Hedley. For a moment, Faro had an unhappy feeling that they were all coming too. With relief he realized it was just another gesture of politeness. Or was it Miss Fortescue's thinly veiled frown of annoyance that quelled all three?

Miss Fortescue waited while Sara Lethie picked up a shawl and draped it about her shoulders. Their backs were turned to Faro but in that moment of stillness he had a strange feeling that uneasy glances were exchanged. Uneasy and warning, perhaps?

And then it was over and Sir Terence was showing them to the door, cordially shaking hands with Faro. Waving them farewell he anxiously regarded the sky.

'Rain's not far off, you're — um, you're going to get wet. Shall I fetch an umbrella?'

'I shall be quite all right,' said Miss Fortescue. She sounded rather cross, and her manner was suddenly that of someone who heartily disliked being fussed over. She set off determinedly at Faro's side.

As they walked through the formal gardens, Faro accommodating his loping stride to her more leisurely pace, he discovered that Miss Fortescue was having problems with her light shoes on the gravel. It occurred to him that she was brave to tackle a walk outdoors at all, especially as the one pair of sturdy, sensible shoes that even ladies-in-waiting to Grand Duchesses might be expected to possess had been lost with her luggage on the night of the accident.

'Shall we keep to the grass, miss? It would be more comfortable for you.'

'It would indeed.' Her smile was grateful.

'What was it you wished to talk to me about?' he asked.

She looked at him wide-eyed. 'How ever did you guess? You are clever.' And as Faro shrugged off the compliment: 'It is such a relief to get you alone. I desperately need to tell you the whole story — as it is coming back to me, quite gradually, of course.'

Her tone warned him not to expect too much. Then halting, she gazed up into his face. 'Quite frankly, Inspector, I am frightened.'

Frightened. He hadn't expected that.

She sighed deeply before continuing. 'I have decided that I must take you into my confidence, Inspector.'

Ah, thought Faro, now we're getting somewhere at last. This could be the break he was waiting for, the thread to lead him through the labyrinth of mystery and misinformation.

'— You see, Amelie wished to keep her journey secret from the President, her husband. She didn't want him to know that she was in fact negotiating with Her Majesty's government to intercede in their problems —'

'May I be permitted to enquire — the nature of these problems?' Faro interrupted.

'I'm not sure . . .' she began vaguely.

Faro stopped walking. 'Look, miss, if I'm to help you and you have decided to trust me, then it is essential that we go right back to the beginning —'

'The beginning,' she echoed, as if that thought had never occurred to her.

'Yes, miss. I'm told that you have been with the Duchess since you were both children and I expect that means you are very close.' He paused. 'And that you share her secrets?' Silence followed this statement. 'Am I right?' he asked gently.

Miss Fortescue sighed.

'Perhaps you know better than anyone else the reasons for her disappearance. Without being aware of it, you may even hold the key to her present whereabouts.'

It was a bold suggestion considering the doleful nature of his own suspicions, but he added encouragingly, 'I gather from what I have heard, officially and from private sources, that Her Highness is a lady of spirit and courage.'

Miss Fortescue laughed. 'Indeed she is. Rumour

has not lied, Inspector.' She looked up at him earnestly. 'Yes, and I am quite sure she would put her trust in you, as I am doing.'

With a sigh she continued: 'You are right, I probably know her better than anyone else, far better than her husband — that odious man —'

'The beginning, miss, if you please.'

'Of course. Amelie is related to both the Queen and Prince Albert, as you probably are aware. She was born on their wedding day, 10 February 1840, and that made her very special to both of them. Indeed, they regarded her sentimentally as their very first child, rather than a mere goddaughter. Their visits to Luxoria were frequent and she came to Windsor Castle with her parents —'

She paused to sigh sadly. 'She adored Uncle Albert, was distraught when he died, and I do believe she was a great comfort to her Aunt Vicky at that time.' She was silent, staring bleakly at the treetops, as if overcome by the memory.

'And you accompanied her on these visits?'

She looked at him blankly for a moment, still lost in that other sad world. 'Some of them.' She sighed. 'When she was seventeen there was a revolution in Luxoria. Such a thing had never happened in its history before. Her bastard cousin Gustav had himself elected President. He knew that by marrying Amelie he would destroy the final opposition. Amelie scorned the idea. She hated him. But he refused to take no for an answer.'

She was silent, walking faster now at his side, as if to escape that distant sorrow.

'And — ?' said Faro.

'He forced himself upon her.' Her voice rose. 'He got her with child so that she had no other option but to marry him. Three months later, a few weeks after their marriage, she miscarried. There will be no other child now. And Gustav needs an heir.'

He smiled. 'She is young still to give up hope.'

'In years, perhaps. But after fifteen years of marriage it seems highly unlikely. Besides, Gustav has a mistress who has recently presented him with a son.'

She paused to allow the significance of that remark to sink in.

'Are you hinting that your mistress might be in danger?' Faro asked. Here at last was a clue, the one undeniable reason for murder. Royal princes throughout history had resorted to the disposal of barren wives by fair means or foul, when presented with an heir, even an illegitimate one.

'Danger?' Miss Fortescue repeated. 'I don't think that has ever entered her mind. Amelie refuses to divorce him, for by so doing, she would relinquish any hope of restoring the Royal party to power. Besides, she has learned through all these dreadful years that personal interests must never be allowed to intrude where her main duty lies. To her country and her people.'

She looked at him. 'Perhaps it is difficult for

you or for anyone not of Royal blood to understand such things, Inspector.'

Faro smiled and shook his head. 'Not for me, miss. I understand perfectly. I know all about duty. It is, or should be, a policeman's first rule. To his sovereign and to the people he serves.'

Miss Fortescue laughed and put a hand on his arm. 'Why, Inspector, we seem to have a great deal in common.' And eyeing him shrewdly. 'I was right, I am sure. Amelie would approve. She would trust you.' With a sigh she went on: 'Knowing how powerful Britain is in world politics, she had some thought that Her Majesty might be able to intercede on her behalf. That by selling some of her jewels she might even be able to raise an army, bring the Royal party back into power.'

'Drastic measures, miss.'

She regarded him dolefully. 'I know. I see now what a mad scheme that was. But, as I said, Amelie is a creature of impulse.'

There was nothing Faro could think of as an appropriate response. Worried by his silence, she said: 'You will respect my confidence, please, Inspector — I must beg of you —'

'Of course, you have my word, miss. I was just wondering about these jewels. Any idea where they might be?'

'Under the waters of the River Forth by now. With all our other possessions,' she said bitterly.

'Including the photograph she was taking to

Her Majesty, I believe.'

'That too.'

'Is there nothing more you can tell me about your mistress? Anything that distinguishes her in particular?'

Miss Fortescue shook her head. 'It is so difficult, Inspector, when you have been with someone every day, practically all your life, to try and say exactly what they look like. There are lots of photographs in the palace at Luxoria, of course.'

And utterly useless by the time they reached Edinburgh, Faro thought grimly. A germ of an idea had grown out of this conversation though. Was it too fantastic, he wondered?

'This coachman. What did he look like?'

'The coachman?' she repeated, surprised by the question. Shaking her head she laughed lightly. 'You know, I haven't the least idea. He just looked like, well, a coachman.'

Faro tried again. 'Was he young or old?'

'Of middle age, I expect,' was the prompt reply.

'Short or tall. Stout or thin?' Faro persisted.

'Middle height.' She looked at Faro's withdrawn expression and added apologetically, 'Well, you see, I only saw him very fleetingly.'

Obviously Faro was expected to know that coachmen, like soldiers and policemen, all looked alike. How foolish of him to expect otherwise. So much for McQuinn's theory that servants had intimate knowledge of one another.

'Had he served long in your mistress's employ?'

Miss Fortescue frowned. 'Oh, no. He merely met us when we disembarked at North Berwick. As a matter of fact, I hardly saw his face.'

Ah, then perhaps his idea wasn't so fantastic after all.

There were now spots of rain, an ominous sky. Faro hoped the approaching storm would contain itself for a little longer.

'I'm truly sorry about the photograph, Inspector. So much was lost that night.' Her sigh made Faro feel just a little ashamed of his concern for what must seem to her of little consequence. There was a slight pause before he asked:

'What was your mistress wearing when the accident happened?'

'Wearing?' Miss Fortescue repeated. 'I think — yes, a woollen travelling cape. Yes, it was violet, her favourite colour, velvet trimmed.'

Progress at last, thought Faro. 'And underneath — ?'

But before Miss Fortescue could reply, the storm broke above their heads, a jagged streak of lightning split the sky, followed by a thunder-clap. The spots of rain turned into a steady flow.

'Oh dear. Oh dear, I must leave you, Inspector. I must run —'

Aware that she could never run anywhere in those slippers, Faro in a gallant gesture removed his cape and slipped it about her shoulders.

Her tender, grateful smile was his reward. 'You are so kind, Inspector, so very kind.'

'You had better hurry, miss.'

'But your cape — you will get wet.'

'I'll get it later. Go — quickly —'

He watched her disappear as the deluge broke, and turning he ran swiftly towards the railway halt, which afforded little shelter beyond an ancient oak tree.

He was greatly relieved to hear the distant sound of a train approaching. By good fortune it was on time, but too late to save him from a drenching.

As the train steamed to a halt, a carriage door was flung open to allow a man to descend to the platform.

The passenger was the historian, Stuart Millar.

Chapter 10

'Why, Inspector Faro. What are you doing here?' Stuart Millar demanded.

Faro explained that he had been visiting the Lethies.

'But you are soaked through, man. You must come back with me.' He pointed. 'That's my cottage over there.'

The guard blew his whistle. Millar put his hand on Faro's arm. 'I won't take no for an answer. Elspeth will have supper ready, I'll get you some dry clothes and you can get the later train.'

Faro considered his wet clothes and the tempting invitation. Tempting and convenient, too, since it would give him a chance to find out what the historian knew about the Lethies and Major Weir.

Millar put up his umbrella and they raced through the rain.

At the cottage, Elspeth was absent. A note said that his supper was in the oven. Taking Faro's coat to the kitchen to be dried, Millar returned with a smoking jacket:

'Put this on. My apologies, Inspector. This is my sister's guild evening. Dear, dear. And I'm playing cards with friends — but never mind. We have an hour or so —'

Faro did not mind in the least. In fact he was grateful for this unique opportunity that the storm had brought his way. It was no difficult task to lead the conversation towards the slums of Edinburgh and the proposed demolition of the West Bow.

'Major Weir? We don't know much about the Major's early life, except that he was born near Carluke and was an officer in the Puritan army in 1641. He served with Montrose during his Covenanting campaign and after the execution of Charles I he retired, settled in Edinburgh and became Captain of the City Guard.'

Millar paused and smiled at him. 'I expect all this is well-known to you. And that the City Guard was not as blameless or efficient as our present-day police force. According to legend, however, it was based on an ancient secret society whose original members were present at the sack of Jerusalem. In the confusion afterwards these respectable Edinburgh citizens ransacked King Solomon's Temple and carried off the portrait of Solomon. There were rumours, however, of more important thefts.'

'Such as?'

'King Solomon's Rod, the staff Moses carried when he received the Ten Commandments and which he used subsequently to divide the waters of the Red Sea to see his people safely over to the land of Egypt. But I digress —'

'You were telling me about this remarkable Major.'

114

'When he retired from the City Guard he became absorbed by spiritual matters. The West Bow was very respectable in his day, occupied by a hard-working and fanatically religious group of tinsmiths, known as the Bowhead Saints. The Major lived there with his sister and became known as Angelical Thomas for his powers of oratory. And according to the records he was never to be seen "in any holy duty without his rod in his hand".

'He had an imposing personality and presence, as well as the gift of the gab. Very tall and saturnine, he always wore a long black cloak. Possessed an astonishing memory too. Could quote reams from the Scriptures and had a genius for leading public prayer, quite irresistible to those who heard him, from all accounts. The staff, he said, was his gift from God, his Holy Rod. It had some strange power, could turn itself into a snake or a serpent, and he was able to work some minor miracles and produce magical effects from rags and powders thrown into the fire.'

'Gunpowder, of course,' said Faro, 'and very impressive for the superstitious. All you are telling me about the Major describes an alchemist who could convince ignorant folk that he was in fact some kind of a minor prophet.'

'Exactly,' said Millar. 'If he had kept it that way, all might have been well. But there was a dark side too. He had one weakness. Ladies could not resist him and he couldn't resist such earthly temptations. Eventually, in his seventies, he took ill, and knowing that his life was near its end, he made an amazing confession of depravity and blasphemy which included a statement that he and his sister had sold their souls to the devil on the road to Musselburgh. This so shocked the authorities that the Lord Provost of Edinburgh summoned the City Guard and thrust them both into the tolbooth for safe-keeping.

'In prison, however, the sister lost her nerve, perhaps knowing all too well the dreadful fate that awaited witches and warlocks, and she implored the bailies to secure the Major's staff. He was, she assured them, powerless without it. But if he were allowed to grasp it then he could drive them all out of doors, regardless of any resistance they might make. She further explained that the devil had given the staff to her brother that momentous day in 1618 when, in exchange for their souls, they were transported to Musselburgh and back again in a coach pulled by six black horses which seemed to be made of fire.

'The Major was burnt at the stake at Greenside in April 1670 — I expect you know it, a village between Leith and Edinburgh. A few days later his sister met the same fate in the Grassmarket. To the end, she was more concerned about her brother's staff than their terrible sentence. When she was told it had been burnt with him, mad with rage, she tore off all her clothes to die stark-naked.'

While Faro listened, a picture was taking shape in his mind. The road to Musselburgh passed through Aberlethie. Destroyed by the Reformation, the priory was in ruins and the Crusader lay on his ravaged tomb.

'The bailie in charge of burning the Major's rod described it as looking like a serpent, hissing like a snake, as it perished. The Major's money was entrusted to his care. He took it home with him and locked it in his study. None of his family slept that night. There were dreadful noises issuing from the locked room, as if the house was going to fall down on them —'

'This bailie,' Faro interrupted. 'Do we know his name?'

Millar smiled. 'Yes. Bailie James Lethie.'

'Lethie!' Faro exclaimed, and Millar nodded.

'In all probability a relation of the present-day family.'

'The original castle — when was it built?'

'Begun in September 1670, completed two years later.'

Surely it was no coincidence that it had been built by that same bailie soon after he had both the magic staff, which he had been entrusted to burn, and the Major's money, too.

No great feat of detection was needed to unravel this two-hundred-year-old mystery. Major Weir's secret was certainly in the staff he carried, and he issued warnings about its supernatural powers in order to keep it safe. Everyone who came in contact with him would be too terrified to steal it.

Intriguing as this information was, Faro decided

that it contributed little to the more urgent matter of solving the mystery of the missing Grand Duchess. He did not greatly relish the prospect of facing an irate Prime Minister and having to give an account of his failure to the Queen herself.

When Faro took his leave of Millar, he decided to walk over to the priory before catching the next train.

The storm had cleared and left in its wake the legacy of a mellow autumn evening with the rich smell of damp earth and a sky, azure and cloudless, echoing with birdsong.

As he looked down at the Crusader's Tomb for the second time that day, his experience was quite different from his earlier visit. Gone was the electric atmosphere which he had interrupted between Miss Fortescue and the two men. Now he felt there was nothing left in this heap of mouldering stone, nothing in this effigy that could help solve his more immediate problem.

The truth or fiction behind the history so colourfully interwoven with legend that had once marked this spot had been lost for ever under the dust and ashes of centuries past.

Often, when Faro stood on a spot where history had been created, he would have given much to be transported back in time for just one brief glimpse of that magic occasion. He could never walk towards the new university on Chambers Street without seeing Kirk o' Field on its site and wishing with all his heart that he could have been there and solved one of Scotland's most tantalizing mysteries.

What had really happened that February night? And was the Queen of Scots implicated in the destruction of her odious husband, Lord Darnley? Now there was only hearsay, dry as dust. But if one could have been there to pick up the clues and prove Mary innocent, then her desperate plight might have changed the whole course of Scotland's history.

Such is the stuff that dreams — or nightmares — are made of. And now, in like manner, Faro wished for a time machine that could carry him back to the scene of David de Lethie returning triumphant from the Crusades, bearing with him a strange trophy.

But tonight he was not the only pilgrim.

Miss Fortescue walked cautiously through the shrubbery. A manservant who had the unfortunate look of a gaoler hovered at a discreet distance, trying to look as if he hadn't been instructed to keep an eye on her.

It was an interesting idea, one which would bear further investigation, Faro thought as he stepped out of the shadow of the priory wall.

As for Miss Fortescue, she was not at all put out by his sudden appearance. She smiled. 'Why, Inspector Faro. I am so glad to see you. I have your cape. It is thoroughly dry now — if you would care to accompany me —' She motioned towards the castle.

'Of course.'

Opening her reticule she handed him a paper. 'I was to have this posted to you, Inspector. It is a list of the contents of the jewel box —'

After a quick glance Faro thrust it into his pocket, as Miss Fortescue continued: 'I hope it helps. It's the best I can do, until Her Highness can confirm the contents.'

Faro found this even more surprising. 'When do you think she is likely to arrive?' he asked politely.

'Oh, I've been thinking it over and I haven't the least doubt that she'll just walk in. Or send us a message from Balmoral. Her Highness is like that. She's very resourceful and impulsive.' She paused to let that sink in. 'But I am most concerned about that poor coachman.'

'Isn't it possible that he may be with her?'

She shook her head. 'I'm afraid that he may have been sent with a message and something has happened to him.' Her eyes filled with tears and she put a hand on his arm, gazing up into his face appealingly. She looked bewildered, overwhelmed by frightening circumstances entirely new in her hitherto sheltered life.

'What do you think we should do meanwhile, Inspector?'

'My colleagues and I are doing all we can to find out what happened. How much do you remember, miss?'

Again she shook her head. 'Only the fierce storm, the carriage swaying. A tree fell. And then — oblivion.'

'What was your last sight of Her Highness?'

'We were clinging to each other.' Her voice broke for an instant. 'The coachman yelled a warning. The bridge is down. I remember falling free of the carriage, rolling down the hill and hitting the water. I thought that was the end as I sank. Then I came to myself, my clothes dripping wet. I was lying on a load of hay. Being carried along a dark road. You know the rest, Inspector.'

He looked at her. 'What are you going to do now? Until such time as your mistress returns for you,' he added hastily.

She shrugged. 'Wait for instructions of some kind. I have no reason to return to Luxoria — if — if —' And in her eyes he read the words neither dared to say, in case by so doing they gave them the breath of life and a monstrous reality.

'What about your family and friends?' he asked gently.

'I have no commitment of any kind. As you probably realize I am not a national.'

'You are British?'

'As Scottish as you are, Inspector,' she said proudly.

Faro bowed, not considering this was the time or place to explain that Orcadians consider themselves a country apart.

'The Queen is, as you know,' Miss Fortescue continued, 'much in favour of Scottish governesses and maids. There are such intimate connections between Her Majesty and most of our Royal houses.'

She fell silent and Faro, anxious to return to the more urgent topic in hand, prompted her: 'When the storm interrupted us you were telling me what your mistress was wearing when the accident happened. A violet travelling cape with velvet trimming, was it not?'

'Yes.'

'And underneath?'

Miss Fortescue frowned. 'A blue merino dress, with long sleeves, an embroidered yoke and a quantity of lace at the neck.'

Faro would have given much at that moment to produce the piece of lace he had found in the West Bow. But the time was not yet ripe. He needed to know a great deal more about the part Miss Fortescue had played before producing such evidence.

'What jewellery was she wearing?'

Miss Fortescue thought. 'A sapphire and diamond ring, gold bracelets.' She rubbed her wrist nervously. 'In the shape of a snake with ruby eyes. No earrings. And a pendant.' And touching her throat. 'Yes, she always wore a pendant. Just a simple gold cross.'

Faro sighed. In that statement, Miss Fortescue was confirming his worst fears.

'And underneath the dress?'

Miss Fortescue was taken aback by the question. She blushed. 'The usual garments ladies wear, Inspector. Petticoats and so forth.'

She sounded offended but Faro persisted. 'Can you be a little more precise, miss?'

'No. I'm afraid I can't,' she said coldly.

Faro gave her a hard look. 'I presume that as lady-in-waiting and sole travelling companion, you were also in charge of her wardrobe and of dressing her each day.'

'I just can't remember, exactly.' She shook her head and pursed her lips firmly, indicating that particular subject was closed.

Faro waited a moment. 'Did she by any chance wear corsets?' he prompted her gently.

'Of course, all ladies wear corsets, Inspector.'

Faro frowned. 'If you are finding this too painful and embarrassing, miss, perhaps you'd be good enough to write it down, as you kindly wrote the jewel-box list. And a drawing would be most helpful if you could manage that.'

'A drawing. I couldn't possibly draw Her Highness,' she said indignantly.

'I meant a drawing of her clothes.'

Miss Fortescue sighed. 'Oh, very well. If I can.'

'If you can, it would be most helpful,' he repeated.

They emerged from the formal garden in silence and both were relieved to find that the castle was in view.

Miss Fortescue's pace quickened and Faro was aware of the servant still keeping them within range. He was desperately searching for some safe conversation when she suddenly said:

'When last we met you were rushing for a train. I presume you missed it.'

'I met Mr Stuart Millar, the historian. He lives on the edge of the estate and I allowed him to persuade me to return to his cottage. He was kind enough to give me supper and a most interesting account of the Crusader and the Luck of Lethie.'

'Oh, indeed,' she said vaguely. 'You would see it when you were staying at the castle, Sir Terence is very proud of it.'

'I had to leave early.' He consulted his watch. 'But perhaps, if I have time — I'm quite curious —'

Miss Fortescue pushed open the front door. 'There is Sir Terence now.'

Sir Terence, thought Faro, was looking mightily relieved to see her. He had the look of an anxious father repressing reproaches to a wayward and obstinate child.

'Inspector Faro would like to see the Luck of Lethie,' she called, and leaving them to it, she ran lightly upstairs.

Sir Terence smiled. 'Our family mascot — come this way.'

Faro followed him into the library.

'This is the oldest part of the house, you will observe the original stone walls.'

He pointed to a niche above the ancient fireplace where a glass case, its velvet backing long devoid of colour, had resting on it a golden horn anchored by metal clips. It was not like any horn Faro had ever seen, resembling a fiery dragon's head, with the mouthpiece at the back of the neck. Its eyes glittered with the blue of sapphires and its scales were embossed with green and red stones which Faro did not doubt were emeralds and rubies.

At his admiring murmur, Sir Terence said: 'Brought back by our Crusader from Jerusalem. According to legend, one of the treasures the Templars stole from King Solomon's Temple after the city fell.' He paused. 'Or so Mr Stuart Millar tells us.'

Faro didn't doubt that there was something in the legend. The horn looked exceedingly old and not a little battered, but if this was the head of Solomon's Rod, then it predated Christianity by a thousand years.

'Could do with a bit of a clean-up,' said Sir Terence apologetically. 'Has hardly left this room since the castle was built in 1670.'

'So it has been carefully preserved by your family for two hundred years. Remarkable.'

'Yes, indeed. We're very superstitious about preserving the Luck o' Lethie.' Sir Terence surveyed it proudly. 'As long as it survives, so will our line continue. It is supposedly a cure for barren women and the only time it has ever been removed from its case was when there were, er, problems.'

His brooding gaze rested suddenly on a painting of himself and Sara and the first five of their eight children. 'Not one of ours, I need hardly add,' he added heartily. 'Our women are never barren.'

Faro, aware of someone behind him, turned to see Miss Fortescue framed in the doorway, his cape over her arm. Her gaze was watchful and she betrayed an air of listening very intently to their conversation.

Thanking them both, Faro announced that he must hurry or he would miss his train.

'Train, Inspector. By no means. You shall have the carriage.' He cut short Faro's protests. 'It is sitting in the coach-house idle, and you have already suffered enough inconvenience for one day. See, it's raining again.'

As they stood together on the front steps, smiling, to wave him goodbye, Faro was not at all displeased to sink into the luxury of the Lethie carriage and be transported home to Newington, where he was greatly looking forward to mulling over the day's events with Vince.

His stepson could be relied upon to be helpful. Vince's suggestions and encouragement were both urgently needed.

Although Faro had, without difficulty but with considerable reliance on his intuition, found a plausible explanation to the two-hundred-year-old mystery of Major Weir's staff and the building of Lethie Castle, a ten-day-old mystery was at present beyond his powers.

Chapter 11

Vince was not at home. Much in need of his stepson's buoyant presence to banish his anguished thoughts, Faro had to wait until breakfast next morning to relate Stuart Millar's story of King Solomon's Rod.

Vince was intrigued, knowing something of the Templars from his Freemason friends. 'I'm told that the oldest Scottish lodge at Kilwinning was founded by Robert the Bruce for the reception of those Knights Templars who had fled from persecution in Europe. A Templars contingent fought at the king's side, you know, on the field at Bannockburn.'

'After inflicting such a crushing victory over King Edward II, one would presume that their future was guaranteed,' said Faro.

'True. But there was more to it than that. Edward's army was considered invincible and some said that this was no normal defeat of a powerful army. Rumour had it that witchcraft and magic were involved —'

Faro laughed. 'Not unknown sentiments for losers to indulge in. They have to have a better excuse than telling their people they just weren't good enough to beat the enemy.'

'I agree. But rumour also claimed that the Templars had some holy relic, which they carried before their king. Certainly it was extraordinary that even in the heat of battle and some fairly bloody hand-to-hand fighting, neither the Bruce nor any of their number suffered a single scratch.'

'Ah!' said Faro.

Vince looked at him quickly. 'You're thinking perhaps it was the Luck o' Lethie. You might be right at that, since the serpent's head goes back to the very origins of the Templars movement. I've often wondered —'

'And what have you wondered?'

'Well, about Solomon's Tower. As you know, it was built on the ruins of a twelfth-century religious house. And that could well have been a Templars chapel. A rich and powerful international brotherhood of religious warriors, Stepfather. Don't let us underestimate them.'

'A secret society so strong that Popes aware of their power had tried to suppress it,' said Faro. 'A society important enough to be taken under the King of Scotland's protection. Gives one food for thought, doesn't it?'

Vince nodded. 'Especially when you now tell me there's a shrine-like upper room in the Mad Bart's cat-ridden establishment. What blasphemy.'

All his training, combined with an extra sense that had served him well in the past, now compelled him to believe that the disappearance of the Grand Duchess was no coincidence, but the outcome of some international intrigue.

As Vince's first patient of the day was announced by Mrs Brook, Faro considered what he hadn't told his stepson.

Was Sir Hedley involved, his pose as an eccentric recluse a screen for less innocent activities?

But aware of Vince's loathing for Sir Hedley, he decided to keep such speculations, as yet wholly without sufficient evidence to support them, to himself.

'I won't be at home tonight, Stepfather. I'm staying at Owen's place. And I must get in a few rounds of golf,' Vince added, with a speculative sigh at a rather threatening sky, 'if I'm to reduce my handicap in time for this Perth tournament.'

Faro smiled. Both he and his stepson seemed doomed to disastrous affairs of the heart. But he felt encouraged that these overnight visits to Cramond, which were becoming more frequent, signalled that Vince might be considering the advocate's pretty sister Olivia as a suitable wife.

At the door, Vince turned. 'Met our cousin Leslie last night. He was at the Spec with some friends and we had a most convivial evening.'

Edinburgh's Speculative Club was famous as a meeting place for graduates where serious matters for discussion were leavened by youthful joviality and high spirits.

'Now that you mention it, you do look as if you might be suffering from a more urgent handicap than the state of your golf,' said Faro.

Vince smiled weakly. 'You miss nothing as usual, Stepfather.'

Faro laughed. 'I also observe that you declined a second helping of Mrs Brook's excellent sausages. Now that is cause for comment. What about Leslie?'

'Tell you about it later. He was Colonel Wrightson's guest.' Vince chuckled enthusiastically. 'What tales he has to tell. Knows everybody who is anybody. Been a guest in practically every noble house the length and breadth of Scotland,' he added in tones of awe. 'Didn't get home till two. Tried to persuade me to go riding with him in the Queen's Park. Rises at six — dear God, what a thought.'

'And what energy,' said Faro.

And as Vince dragged himself off, still yawning, to his surgery, Faro hoped, for their own sakes, that all his patients were reasonably healthy that day.

Shortly afterwards, as Faro was closing his front door, the familiar police carriage rattled round the corner.

A young policeman leapt down and saluted smartly.

'Constable Burns, sir. Glad I caught you, sir. Man out walking his dogs found a man's body in the shrubbery by St Anthony's Chapel. Dr Cranley's there. Wants a word with you before moving the body.'

Faro jumped into the carriage with an ominous

feeling of disaster. In reply to his question the Constable shook his head.

'No, there wasn't any identification.'

'Any signs of violence?'

'Nothing that a quick look would reveal.' The Constable gave a grimace of distaste. 'Been there some time, I'd say.'

Another mysterious corpse. Was this the missing coachman?

'Indeed. Have you seen anything unusual — any reports of disturbance in the area?'

'Nothing, sir. My beat is in that area of the park with Constable Reid. We don't usually patrol Arthur's Seat or Salisbury Crags yard by yard, unless we have special instructions to do so,' he added anxiously. 'I expect the dead man was taken with a heart attack.'

Like the Grand Duchess, Faro thought grimly as they left the carriage and set off on foot up the steep bank which overlooked Holyroodhouse. The Palace's extensive gardens were now grey and empty, the trees stripped bare. A melancholy wind came from the sea beyond Salisbury Crags hurling before it heavy clouds, towards a skyline dominated by Edinburgh Castle and the High Street's tall houses.

Ahead of them lay the ruins of St Anthony's Chapel. There, according to tradition, a hermit had once tended the chapel altar and kept a light burning in the tower to guide mariners safely up the River Forth. Built in the fifteenth century, a hospice for those afflicted with 'St Anthony's

Fire' — epilepsy — the chapel guarded the Holy Well whose pagan origins predated the Abbey of Holy Rood, site of King David I's encounter with a magical stag bearing a cross between its antlers.

Faro paused to look back at the loch gleaming far below. A peaceful scene of swans gliding in majestic serenity untroubled by the follies of men, he thought, staring at the group of tiny figures who bustled back and forth high above.

The corpse was half-hidden by shrubbery. Dr Cranley, Sergeant McQuinn and Constable Reid hovered nearby. And at a safe distance, looking rather green, was the man who had made the discovery.

Introduced as Mr Innes, Faro recognized him as a Newington shopkeeper. Middle-aged, well-to-do, Innes was clearly unused to such dramas threatening the sanctity of his early morning constitutional. He wore a look of outraged respectability that he should have found himself in the undignified predicament of discovering a body and having to associate with the police.

'It was Daisy found him.' Innes pointed accusingly towards a small bright-eyed Skye terrier. Possessor of the only nose quite unoffended by the stench of decomposition, Daisy looked proud enough to burst. Overcome by a fury of tail-wagging and seizing every opportunity to dash forward, she whined softly, eyeing the body with the proprietary and almost predatory relish of a dog prevented from further demolishing a particularly succulent bone.

Mr Innes was much embarrassed by such ill-bred behaviour and Daisy was frequently called to heel, rewarding her master with gentle-eyed reproach. When she was finally put on her chain she continued to whine in protest, deprived and ill-treated and looking as down in the mouth as a canine could manage.

Mr Innes wasn't looking particularly happy either.

'When will I be allowed to return home?' he asked.

'I requested that he remain here until you arrived,' Dr Cranley called across to Faro, neatly side-stepping the responsibility.

'My wife will be anxious.' Mr Innes consulted his watch. 'I have already missed breakfast and we have a business to run.'

McQuinn came over and said to Faro: 'Constable Burns came for me, I've taken a statement from the gentleman.'

'In that case, sir, we need detain you no longer,' said Faro.

Innes turned to leave, took a few steps and changed his mind. Pointing to the body, he said to Faro, 'However long that — that — has been here, it certainly wasn't there last night.'

'Are you sure?' asked Faro.

'Certain sure. This is our evening walk, regular as clockwork and in most weathers too. It's Daisy's favourite. She's a great ratter and is always in that shrubbery after them, sniffing around. I can vouch for that, if necessary.'

Faro took the card Innes handed him, and thanking him for his help he watched them depart, the man relieved, the dog dragged reluctantly from her scene of triumph. Her reproachful whimpers indicated that this was what a dog's life was all about.

Dr Cranley, who had been bending over the corpse, strode towards Faro. Removing the handkerchief covering his nose and mouth, he said: 'Thought you'd better have a look before we move him.' He shook his head. 'This was no heart attack. Can't tell until we do the postmortem but, at a rough guess, I'd say he most likely drowned.'

'Drowned?'

'Yes, drowned.'

'When?' Faro demanded sharply.

'More than a week ago, I'd estimate.'

'Which fits in with what Mr Innes suggested,' said McQuinn. 'That the body wasn't here last night. Probably dumped a few hours ago.'

Dr Cranley nodded. 'I'd say he was right about that.' He jerked his head in the direction of the loch far below. 'Probably down there.'

'So where has he been all this time?' Faro demanded. 'He certainly didn't get up here unaided.'

The doctor shrugged. 'That's your business, Faro. Mine is restricted to the facts regarding the cause of death, not his whereabouts since death occurred.'

Faro hardly listened. He was a very worried man. The significance of the time-lapse was ominous, it slotted almost too neatly into the grim discovery in the West Bow.

The two fatalities he felt sure were unlikely to be coincidental.

'Any identification?'

'None. Pockets empty.'

Faro sighed like a man whose worst fears have come to pass as he followed Cranley, who said: 'You'll need to cover up.'

And as Faro withdrew a handkerchief from his pocket, Dr Cranley continued: 'It's not a pleasant sight. Damn rum business, I'd say, in more ways than meets the eye.'

The doctor was strongly addicted to rum and clichés and Faro would have appreciated a less sensitive nose as well as a fortifying strong drink as he looked down on the remains of a middle-aged man. Of middle height and middle build, no longer with any features of distinction except for thinning ginger hair, his clothes worn but respectable, his description when circulated, Faro decided wearily, might fit one-quarter of the male population of Scotland.

McQuinn had been listening attentively to the conversation between the doctor and Faro. 'If he drowned down there, sir, why carry him all this way uphill to leave him in the shrubbery? It doesn't make sense.'

Faro sighed. 'His body was obviously concealed somewhere.'

'Not in the open air, that's for sure,' said the doctor. 'Animals would have got at him and there would have been maggot infestation by now.'

'There's been a lot of rain and his clothes would have been ruined too,' said Faro, examining the man's hands. Smooth, with no callouses, not the hands of a labouring man. And whatever his occupation, the dead man had not been a professional coachman with palms hardened by daily contact with horses' reins.

Watching Faro, Cranley said: 'He wasn't in the water long. Was that what you're looking for?'

Faro nodded. Within a few hours of being immersed in water the skin on the hands and feet of a dead body takes on a characteristic bleached and wrinkled appearance, commonly known as 'washerwoman's hands'.

'We'll see what the post-mortem reveals. But I can tell you one thing. I'd be prepared to swear that he's been kept in a closed dry place since he died.'

'Such as?'

Cranley shrugged. 'A trunk, or a closet,' he said grimly. 'Or some airless space, like a cupboard. Well, well, here's another little mystery for you to work on, Faro. If you want my opinion on this one — although I don't suppose we'll find any marks of violence — I won't be surprised if there was foul play involved somewhere.'

When Faro didn't respond, he continued: 'I expect you'll have to complete the usual enquiries before we dispose of the corpse.'

The doctor managed a wry smile. 'Not as much use to our students as the last one we had from you,' he added appreciatively, as if Faro was somehow reponsible for the personal freshness of the corpses supplied to his medical students.

Faro had an unhappy feeling that they would get no further with the dead man in St Anthony's Chapel than they had with the mystery woman in the West Bow. But he would very much have liked an answer to one vital question.

According to Miss Fortescue's account of the events, the coachman who drove the Duchess from North Berwick had probably drowned when the carriage went into the river. Had the accident been prearranged and the coachman murdered, his body concealed for nearly two weeks to be resurrected and left at St Anthony's Chapel on the slopes of Arthur's Seat?

But why, when there were so many less tortuous ways a corpse could be disposed of? With plenty of water around, the River Forth was an obvious choice. Hopefully the body might drift out with the tide and never be seen again.

What was the purpose behind this sudden resurrection? he asked himself as he watched the body being bundled on to a stretcher and carried down the hill by the two constables in the wake of Dr Cranley.

McQuinn remained with him, and now that the corpse had been removed, there was further evidence that its sojourn in the shrubbery had been brief. The leaves and grass where the body had lain were flattened but there was none of the yellow discoloration and decay that would have occurred had the vegetation been covered for several days.

'I had a walk round, sir, nothing to be seen out of the ordinary,' McQuinn added.

As Faro poked round the shrubbery with a stick and without much hope of finding anything significant, he smelt murder as well as decomposition in the air.

McQuinn frowned. 'It's only a thought, sir, but the fact that the man was drowned — well, do you think there could be a link with the missing Duchess?'

'I think there's a very strong possibility that they are connected.'

McQuinn nodded. 'Pity the newspapers couldn't produce a photograph of her. That would have been a great help. One thing I don't understand though, why keep the body — for a week?'

Faro would dearly have loved the answer to that question. All it indicated to him was that the assassin was getting nervous.

Of the Grand Duchess's entourage, only Miss Fortescue now remained alive.

But for how long?

Chapter 12

As Faro and McQuinn emerged from the shelter of the ruined chapel and prepared to rejoin the police carriage, they were hailed by a figure toiling up the hill.

It was Leslie Godwin, leading a horse, and on the path below, Sergeant Batey.

'Shall I wait, sir?' said McQuinn.

'No. You head back.'

Leslie approached Faro eagerly. 'I'm out later than usual. Missed my early morning ride.' He gave his cousin a quizzical glance. 'I expect Vince will have told you. We had a somewhat convivial evening at the Spec.'

Faro smiled. No doubt Leslie's tough and dangerous existence through the years made him impervious to the excesses of high living. Although considerably older than Vince, Faro decided that his cousin was also in better shape than either of them.

As they watched the forlorn cavalcade descending the hill with their stretcher, Leslie explained: 'Saw your policemen gathered and —' He grinned. 'You know me — I decided there must be a story. As soon as I spotted you, I knew I was right. So here I am.' He sat down on a nearby rock, anchoring his horse's reins.

'Well, what have you got to tell me?' At Faro's stern expression, he laughed. 'Not another mysterious corpse, I trust.'

When Faro frowned, his cousin's eyes widened. 'That was meant as a joke — not in the best of taste, I realize.'

Faro received this observation in silence and Leslie whistled. 'Some connection between the two, eh. Well, now.'

Faro couldn't think of a reply and Leslie continued sternly, 'Come now, Jeremy, don't you think it's time you brought me into this? You know I want to help and, who knows, maybe I can —'

'There isn't anything —' Faro began hastily.

Leslie held up his hand. 'Please don't try to fob me off, I'm an old hand at the game,' he added in wounded tones. 'Besides, I know that you are involved in what might turn out to be a scandalous piece of international intrigue.'

Faro felt suddenly chilled. 'And what makes you think that?'

Leslie smiled. 'From hints dropped — confidentially, of course — at the Spec last night,' he added with an impish smile, 'I gathered that none other than the Grand Duchess of Luxoria has gone amissing.'

Damn Vince. Drink loosened his tongue. He had never learned to control that particular student weakness. Damn him, Faro thought angrily as Leslie continued:

'And I suddenly realized that this is where I

might be able to help you.'

'In what way?'

'The best possible.' Leslie regarded him triumphantly. 'You see, I've been to Luxoria. A couple of years ago when I was travelling across Europe, I had the honour to be received by members of the Royal family —'

This was an unexpected piece of luck. Faro looked at him gratefully. 'You met the Grand Duchess.'

Leslie shook his head. 'Alas, no, she was absent, if you please, with her husband, the odious President. As nasty a situation as anyone could imagine, a piece of emotional blackmail worthy of grand opera.'

'How so?'

'I got the general drift, that her family had literally sold her to save their skins, whatever they were pretending. You don't know the story?'

Faro did but he wanted to hear his cousin's version, which confirmed exactly what Miss Fortescue had confided in him. Then he added: 'He'd like to divorce Amelie and marry his mistress — if that wouldn't mean the end of his power.'

It was even worse than Faro had thought. The President had very good reason for disposing of the Grand Duchess, and a professional assassin could easily be bought for the kind of money the ruthless President was prepared to pay.

As they stumbled through the bracken, the short cut to the road far below, Faro turned and asked with sudden hope:

'Did you by any chance see any photographs of her?'

Leslie thought for a moment. 'I was only there very briefly, a few days. Hardly enough to do more than take a passing interest in my surroundings. There were some family paintings on the walls, sentimental reminders of the Royal Family in their heyday — But seventeen-year-old girls can change quite a bit with the passing years — not to mention an unhappy marriage.'

'But there is a possibility you might recognize her again?'

Leslie laughed. 'I don't know what you're getting at, but yes, I've got quite a good memory for faces, and if the setting was right, I suppose.' He paused, then added, 'There's a strong family resemblance to the House of Hanover and the Saxe-Coburgs. Hardly surprising since they're all related. And let's not forget that artists who know when they're on to a good thing, tend to err on the side of flattery.'

He looked hard at Faro. 'What are you getting at, Jeremy?' And when his cousin didn't answer, he indicated a large boulder and sitting down on it made a place for Faro. Then smiling encouragingly, he said gently: 'Why not start at the beginning? Who was the last person to see the Grand Duchess?'

'Her lady-in-waiting, Miss Fortescue —'

'And where is she now?'

'At Lethie Castle —'

Leslie listened carefully, frowning occasionally as Faro told him the events of the disastrous landing at North Berwick and Miss Fortescue's flight to Solomon's Tower.

At the end, Leslie sighed, his only comment: 'Vanished into thin air. Just like that.'

Before replying, Faro said a silent prayer that his fears were groundless. 'I take it that the corpse in the West Bow that night didn't strike you in any way as familiar.'

'Familiar?' Leslie stared at him. Then as realization dawned, he whispered: 'You mean — you think —'

'Well, could it?'

'Oh lord, Jeremy. I don't know. I haven't the foggiest. I didn't look at her very closely. You know how it is.' He looked thoughtful. 'Have you considered that another talk with the lad Sandy might be useful? It could well be that he's hiding something.'

And studying Faro, he shrugged. 'I'm no detective, you know, but right from the start the lad's manner struck me as suspicious.'

'That he was plain scared, you mean.' Faro smiled. 'It isn't every day that a twelve-year-old lad stumbles on a corpse. Or finds himself surrounded by the police.'

'I agree. It could be that the scent of the law so near home put him off. Most of these lads live by dubious activities, and as you know Batey grabbed him by the ear, with his hand in my pocket.'

He laughed. 'Quite brazen about it, he was too. Yes, I think you would be well-advised to have a talk. And it would help if you had a coin or two in hand. Nothing like the sight of money for lubricating information.'

'I have tried,' said Faro. 'Called at the house when I left you the other day.'

'Well?'

'He wasn't at home, but I left a message with his mother and the promise of two shillings.'

Leslie nodded eagerly. 'That should bring him running to your door.'

They got up and walked on in silence for a few moments before Leslie turned and added: 'If in doubt, you could have the corpse exhumed.'

'I'm afraid not. There is no resurrection for this particular corpse. All unknown and unclaimed bodies become the property of Dr Cranley and his students.'

'Dear God. You mean —' And Leslie made a grisly gesture of using a knife.

'Precisely.'

'How awful.'

And as if in accompaniment to grim realization, they reached the park road pursued by rain sheets that crept steadily over the hill, shrouding Arthur's Seat in thunderheads. The sky rumbled ominously in the grip of an approaching storm, reminding Faro that this swiftly changing weather signalled golden autumn would soon be replaced by dark November. Cold winter days, where early darkness made petty crime more profitable and detection a hundred times more difficult and un-comfortable.

On the road, Sergeant Batey was waiting. He helped his master to mount, looking neither to left nor to right. Faro might not have existed, nor McQuinn standing a few yards away.

Batey's behaviour made Faro uneasy. There was something unhuman about him, an attitude he had only ever met in the most hardened criminals, killers by inclination rather than by the circumstances that make men into soldiers.

He looked at his cousin Leslie, so open-faced and frank, at the handsome Irish McQuinn and was struck by the comparison. Batey might be a good servant perhaps, but not one Faro would have cared to keep under his roof.

Leslie waved a cheerful farewell with a promise to meet again soon. Winking broadly at his cousin, he called: 'You've given me plenty to think about. I'll let you know if I come up with any brilliant ideas.'

Faro watched the two men, so completely dis-similar, gallop back towards the Canongate. Then turning he surveyed the ruined chapel thought-fully. The sloping foothills of Arthur's Seat were almost deserted, except for one other domestic building, almost as ancient as the chapel itself.

Solomon's Tower. Not very far away, in fact quite conveniently accessible and offering splendid opportunities for hiding a body. With or without the Mad Bart's knowledge or consent, he thought grimly.

Narrowing his eyes, he remembered Miss Fortescue half-alive, staggering into the Tower, her story not quite the same as the one the Mad Bart had produced. And on the off-chance of finding him at home, he decided to call and direct a few searching questions on what had really happened that night.

He was unlucky. There was no human response to the clanging bell which, however, alerted the feline inhabitants. As he opened the door, he was engulfed in a purring tide of cats, all intent on insinuating themselves about his ankles. Faro no longer had any worries that Sir Hedley might be lying dead in his cat-haunted tower. So, restraining them from escaping into the garden, and having endured enough strong and unpleasant odours for one day, he beat a hasty retreat.

Before going out to Aberlethie to see if Miss Fortescue could shed any light on the identity of the corpse in St Anthony's Chapel, Faro had decided to make certain that the dead man was not already on the Edinburgh City Police's missing persons list.

At the Central Office, Sergeant McQuinn had forestalled him. He shook his head. 'No one even resembling him, sir.'

'You're quite sure?'

Faro was surprised, having expected several missing men of similar ordinariness whose descriptions might roughly fit the one he now thought of as the missing coachman.

'I'll make the usual routine enquiries, sir, but it looks as if we might be landed with a Mr Nobody.'

The missing persons list was not, Faro knew, completely reliable. For every person who disappeared and was urgently sought by relatives for reasons of love or loathing or by creditors for lucre, there were dozens more husbands and wives, sons and daughters who disappeared discreetly and whose relatives for their own reasons kept silent. If enquiries had been made, doubtless the police would have found that these same people were grateful to see the last of their missing relative, saying their prayers each night that they might never again be troubled by the sound of that dreaded footfall crossing their threshold.

'We've had the list of the contents of the Duchess's jewel box distributed, sir. None of the pieces have turned up with any of the legitimate dealers.'

'It's early days for that. How about some of the illicit ones?' Even as he spoke, Faro realized the hopelessness of such a task. Fences would be hanging on to them for a month or two until the scent grew cold, or trying to sell them on the continent for quick disposal.

More than an hour had passed since Faro and McQuinn had left the scene on the road below St Anthony's Chapel.

On the off-chance that Dr Cranley had made a discovery of some importance they went together to the mortuary where, having just completed his grisly business, the doctor was washing his hands.

Giving Faro a triumphant look, he said: 'I was right, you know, he was drowned. His lungs had ballooned as a result of distension with water. That's how he died, but he wasn't in the water for long —'

As Dr Cranley proceeded to reiterate what Faro knew already, he listened politely, then took his leave.

Outside, McQuinn said, 'Looks as if we have a murder enquiry on our hands, sir.'

'I'm afraid so.' Faro looked at his watch. 'Take care of the preliminary business, will you, McQuinn. I'm off to Aberlethie — there's a train to North Berwick in half an hour. I want to talk to Miss Fortescue again.'

'You think she may know something?'

'My thoughts are leading steadily in that direction, McQuinn. Something vital to the case, that she doesn't even realize she knows until she's prompted and it surfaces into her memory again.'

McQuinn looked at him frowning. 'You think the dead man might be the missing coachman?'

'I am fairly certain of that, at least.'

As Faro was leaving the Central Office, Constable Reid came up the steps. 'A burglary inside the Castle, sir.'

'Civilian?'

'Yes, sir.'

'You take care of it —'

The Constable looked uncomfortable. 'Colonel Wrightson asked to see you specially, sir. Urgent, he said it was.'

'Very well.' Constable Reid's cape gleamed with rain, and as Faro looked with little enthusiasm upon the downpour, the Constable said encouragingly, 'I'll get you a carriage, sir.'

Five minutes later, the police carriage was toiling up the High Street and the Esplanade, transformed into twin rivers of brown water and debris from overflowing gutters.

At the Castle, he was escorted to the Colonel's private apartments. Wrightson was waiting for him. He smiled apologetically.

'Nothing serious, Faro. Nothing to worry about. Do sit down. Have a drink.'

Faro did as he was bid and with a whisky in hand tried to suppress his impatience. He had too much on his mind to be in a mood for the trifling details of a break-in at the Castle that any of his constables could have dealt with efficiently.

'. . . in this room, but nothing was taken, as far as we can see,' the Colonel went on. 'In fact, we wouldn't have known that there had been a break-in except that the man was spotted leaving the room. He wasn't in uniform and when challenged, took to his heels. It was then my man gave the alert. I came immediately —'

Faro was looking round the room. With trophies on every shelf, every inch of wall space

occupied by paintings and army group photographs, it would be extremely difficult at first
glance to know if anything was missing. His glance
wandered to the massive desk, awash with books
and documents.

Wrightson followed his gaze and nodded. 'I suspect that the desk was the target.'

At Faro's questioning look, he continued, 'Well,
there was one drawer — over here.'

Faro saw that the lock bore marks of a sharp
instrument being used on it. 'Is there anything
missing?'

Wrightson wriggled uncomfortably. 'That I
can't honestly say.'

Faro looked at him. 'Surely you know what
the drawer contained, sir.' And when the Colonel
looked blank, he prompted: 'Documents, for instance, perhaps of a secret or confidential nature?'

The Colonel laughed. 'No. That's what's so
odd. I think he must have broken open the wrong
drawer. There are such papers — here — and
here —' He indicated several drawers. 'But this
one is where I keep my mementoes and stationery.
Everything relating to my years serving Her Majesty at Holyrood, I just thrust in there. Not a
bit of use to anyone, that I can assure you.'

'Nothing of value, then? You are certain of
that?'

The Colonel smiled. 'Only to me. You see, Faro,
I'm a bit of a hoarder, can't bear to throw any-
thing away. I kept all the menus, notes from
Her Majesty, memos — ribbons off cakes. Ev-

erything and all purely sentimental things.'

'You wouldn't by any chance have a list of the contents?' Even as he asked Faro realized that was a forlorn hope.

At his bleak expression, Wrightson shook his head. 'I'm not a list man. I'm sorry, Faro, I've really wasted your time,' he added apologetically.

'Not at all, sir,' said Faro gallantly, as he considered that was precisely what Wrightson had done. 'Who has access to these rooms, sir?'

'None of my men, if that's what you mean. There's tight security about that. Officers' quarters, strictly out of bounds.'

'So none of them could come in here without your knowledge?'

The Colonel shook his head. 'Or without my batman. He accompanies any soldier — or officer — who has reason to seek an interview. And they wouldn't be left alone by him, not for a minute, if that's what you're hinting at.'

'Have there been any such interviews recently?'

'None at all.'

'When was the last time this room was occupied by other than yourself and your batman, sir?'

Wrightson thought for a moment. 'The other evening, at the dinner party. Why, you were here, Faro. Remember, we all had drinks before going in.'

Faro shook his head. 'I missed that part of the proceedings, sir. Unavoidably detained, I arrived late.'

Wrightson gave him an indignant look. 'Wait

151

a moment, Faro. What are you getting at? Not suggesting that one of my guests would go through my desk when my back was turned — I hope.'

'I'm only saying that your friends are the only persons with access to this room apart from your batman.'

'Well!' Wrightson gave a shout of indignation. 'I don't have those kind of friends, that I can assure you, sir. The very idea.' Suddenly speechless, he continued to regard Faro angrily, his face scarlet, outraged by such a suggestion.

'It's my duty to ask such questions, sir, unpleasant though they may be for you,' Faro added in what he hoped was a mollifying tone. 'I'm not insulting your friends, merely endeavouring to investigate the burglary you have reported.'

'I see, I see,' said Wrightson impatiently.

'I need to know whether you've had anything of value stolen. The man who was apprehended might well have been a civilian who sneaked in out of curiosity — or bravado — got lost and found himself in this part of the Castle —'

But even as he said it, as he hoped in firm and convincing tones, Faro didn't believe it and neither, he suspected, did Wrightson, although he was prepared to accept this as a possible explanation.

As Faro rose to leave, the Colonel said, 'My apologies for bringing you here on a wild-goose chase.'

'Not at all, sir. If civilians are involved then it is our business to protect you.'

Wrightson thought for a moment. 'I did wonder at first, if this might have something to do with that other attempted break-in — from the outside. Remember, Faro, more than a week ago?'

The same thought had been in Faro's mind. He could see no connection between the two events but the idea was vaguely disturbing.

He left the Castle feeling that he would much rather have had a proper burglary to investigate, with a few silver trophies taken and a few clues to follow, than an apparently motiveless petty crime.

The possibility of a passerby overcome by curiosity was too remote and yet oddly sinister in its simplicity. Secret and confidential documents for sale to foreign powers seemed the most plausible reason.

Faro sighed. At least with silver trophies and items of value, there existed a list at the Edinburgh City Police of what they called 'the usual suspects', criminals to be rounded up from the notorious warrens of Wormwoodhall in Causewayside. But from their number, few violent men would risk breaking into the well-guarded officers' quarters in the Castle merely to open a drawer in Wrightson's desk full of sentimental Royal mementoes. This certainly did not bear the mark of any of the city's well-kenned criminal hierarchy who all left recognizable trademarks.

As the carriage headed towards Waverley Station through the torrential rain, Arthur's Seat was obliterated by mist. Faro wished the incidents of that morning could as readily be dissolved, but one thought in particular refused to be banished.

Was it significant that Miss Fortescue had suggested that the coachman had drowned? Did she know a great deal more about the events of that night than she was prepared to disclose? If so, in common with those who knew too much about assassins, she might well be in mortal danger.

Chapter 13

'Not another train till six o'clock, sir,' said the railway guard cheerfully, as Faro dashing to the barrier watched the North Berwick train steaming out of the station.

Slowed down by the appalling condition of flooded roads from the Castle, he'd missed it by seconds. And now he made the discovery that his boots were leaking. This damned rain!

Leaving the empty platform, cursing Edinburgh's foul weather, he decided he might as well return to the Central Office and log his interview with Colonel Wrightson about the break-in. He set off at a brisk pace towards the High Street to be caught in yet another downpour.

'Where in damnation is it all coming from?' he demanded of McQuinn, who was leaving in the police carriage, heading for Liberton. The young sergeant took pity on his bedraggled appearance.

'Why don't you get some dry clothes, sir — we'll drop you off at the house.'

Faro was glad to accept, and as they drove in the direction of Newington, in answer to his question, McQuinn said:

'Nothing new to report, sir. Thought you were going to Aberlethie?'

'There was an attempted break-in at the Castle —'

As Faro related his meeting with the Colonel, McQuinn listened sympathetically.

'Doesn't sound like one of our lads, sir. Doubt if rounding them up would do any good.'

'Complete waste of time, I'd say,' Faro agreed.

Opening his front door a few minutes later, Faro realized that the house was unusually silent without Mrs Brook's bustling presence. Her niece was getting married in Dundee and she had been persuaded, very much against her will, to take a couple of days off.

Swept off balance by a false step on the hall carpet, he cursed again, sniffing the air. Mrs Brook refused to take seriously his warnings about highly polished floors. Certain that the whole structure of 9 Sheridan Place would collapse in her absence and her two gentlemen die of neglect, she had once again been over-generous with the beeswax.

Changing his boots and taking the damp ones down to the kitchen, Faro looked into the larder. It was filled to overflowing with covered and labelled dishes complete with neatly written menus for each meal.

He stood back, exasperated by such efficiency. He deplored waste, and the prospect of tackling what appeared to be enough provisions for a whole regiment on a month-long siege, made him feel guilty.

The room was suddenly lit by a flash of lightning. As thunder rumbled angrily back and forth across the sky, like a dialogue between two ill-tempered giants, Faro gave up any idea of travelling to Aberlethie and back again. He had had quite enough for one day. Tomorrow morning his best boots would be dry, and hopefully the rain which had persisted all day would have worn itself out with its continued efforts.

The decision made, he sat down at the kitchen table with a slice of cold pork pie before him, suddenly charmed at the novelty of having the house to himself. He couldn't remember the last time, if ever, this agreeable experience had occurred.

Discovering that he had an appetite and was hungrier than usual at this hour of the day, he was attacking a second slice of Mrs Brook's excellent fruit cake when the front doorbell clanged through the house.

As it jangled noisily a second time, he decided to ignore it. Doubtless some tradesman was seeking Mrs Brook. Resentful at having his peaceful meal interrupted by this intrusion he was taking another bite of cake when conscience told him that the caller might be a patient in urgent need of Dr Laurie's attention.

In Vince's absence, such cases were referred to a retired colleague in Minto Street. Now where was the card?

The doorbell had clanged vigorously a third time when he found it on the mantelpiece, and hoping he wasn't too late, he ran upstairs.

On the doorstep, he was taken aback to find, not a frantic patient, but Miss Fortescue.

'I'm so glad to find you at home, Inspector. I called at the Central Office and they told me you had left —'

She was obviously very agitated, staring back over her shoulder, nervously searching the street in the manner of one who suspects she is being followed. And Faro almost expected to see the Lethie servant hovering at a discreet distance.

'I had to see you, Inspector.'

'Won't you come in?'

Her travelling cape was almost as wet as her umbrella. He wondered if this was a planned departure from Lethie Castle — the word 'escape' came to his mind unheeded, for she carried a straw-lidded travelling basket, the kind favoured by ladies on short summer expeditions.

Releasing her from her cape he said: 'I'll take this down to the kitchen, miss. It'll soon dry out on the stove.'

As Mrs Brook's highly polished floor threatened to claim its second victim, he seized her elbow, apologized and pointed her in the direction of the drawing-room: 'Take a seat if you please, miss. I'll be with you directly.'

He put out his hand for the travelling bag. Shaking her head firmly she smiled up at him.

'I'm sorry to be a nuisance. I did get rather wet waiting for a carriage at the station. They were all claimed immediately they arrived. I'm afraid I haven't quite the knack of rushing forward and arguing with strong men brandishing stout walking-sticks.'

'It's always like that in bad weather, miss,' said Faro, surprised that she hadn't come in the Lethie carriage.

When he said so, she shook her head. 'No, I came by train. I left them a note. You see, Inspector, I'm quite desperate. I really cannot bear things to go on — in this uncertainty. I'm not a very patient person. I must take matters into my own hands. And do something,' she emphasized.

It all seemed very courageous, thought Faro, but hardly what he expected. And more important, what precisely did she expect him to do? He had problems enough without a distressed lady-in-waiting on his hands.

'I need hardly tell you, Inspector, I am utterly weary of sitting out there at Lethie listening to Terence and Sara assuring me that everything is going to be all right.'

She looked at him steadily and added slowly, 'When I am absolutely sure now that something has gone terribly wrong. Otherwise, news of some sort should have reached me by now. Don't you agree?' And without waiting for his answer:

'Of course, the dear Lethies have been so good and kind. They're very patient and conscientious, especially as they are leaving for a family wedding in Paris at the end of the week.'

Pausing, she regarded him helplessly. 'We haven't discussed what will happen to me in their absence, what arrangements they have made.'

What indeed, thought Faro. She could hardly be returned to Solomon's Tower and the hospitality of Sir Hedley Marsh, that was for sure.

'I felt I couldn't just sit in that empty house a moment longer,' she continued, shaking her head vigorously, 'I am used to an active life, you know. Routine, and all that sort of thing. I must confess, I am terribly bored by all this enforced idleness — sitting waiting for news is very disagreeable for one's nerves. Each time a servant comes in or a rider appears on the drive, one's hopes are raised and then dashed severely to the ground again. I feel like a prisoner, waiting to be released.'

She sighed, looking at him expectantly.

Faro's murmur of sympathy seemed to encourage her and she went on: 'While they were out visiting this morning, I decided I must try to — well, escape for a while. I was so longing to see something of your lovely city. So I left them a note and caught the train at the halt.' Staring ruefully at the streaming windows, she added: 'I hadn't bargained for the weather, of course. It was dull but still fair when I left this morning.'

As Faro listened he was grateful for the missed train to North Berwick that had saved him a futile visit to Lethie Castle.

'— I've had a perfectly splendid day,' Miss Fortescue went on. 'Princes Street is a delight, such lovely shops. And I didn't mind getting wet. Rain like this is something of a rarity in Luxoria. And we are never allowed to get wet —'

Faro was wondering how he was expected to respond to this burst of enthusiasm when she sighed deeply, troubled no doubt by thoughts of her Royal friend and companion.

'We're all doing as much as we can, miss, to find your mistress,' he reminded her gently.

Straightening her shoulders, she said sternly, 'And that is precisely why I am here, Inspector. I am absolutely certain that she must have reached Her Majesty by now. That was the prime intention of this visit. Lethie was to be an overnight stay only, renewing old acquaintance with — with my family who have served hers so well. Why then has there been no word to them — or to me? She is such a thoughtful person, I assure you. She cares deeply about her friends and those who serve her.'

Again she looked at Faro, who could think of no answer beyond nodding in agreement.

'I keep thinking of her sitting in Balmoral Castle — at this very moment, Inspector, perhaps believing that I was drowned that awful night. Do you think it is possible, as I suggested to you, that she has sent word to Lethie Castle and some misfortune has befallen the messenger? Have you any means of finding out?'

When Faro didn't respond, she put a beseeching hand on his arm. 'I must find her. Please, Inspector — you must take me to her. She will

161

be so relieved to know that I am unharmed.'

Faro stared at her, at a loss for appropriate words. Or any words, in fact. His hesitation was mistaken and she went on hastily:

'Oh, I'm not reproaching you in any way, Inspector, please don't think that. I do regard your efforts most highly. I'm sure you have our best interests at heart. Indeed,' she added with an engagingly shy smile, 'I think of you as a friend almost.'

Faro bowed, and playing for time and some suitable response to Miss Fortescue's proposal, he removed the fire-guard and attempted to light the fire which Mrs Brook had set in readiness. As it smoked dismally, he said: 'I'll just go and see how your cape is drying, miss. If you'll excuse me.'

She smiled. 'I imagine that your wife is used to such weather and dealing with emergencies like drying wet garments.'

'I'm not married, miss.'

'Oh, I'm sorry.' She looked round with a puzzled frown. 'Then you have a very good housekeeper, this room has a woman's touch.'

'That is so. This is her day off. However, I shall endeavour to make you a cup of tea.'

Having put on the kettle, he returned to find her looking out of the window. 'This is such a pretty house, Inspector. I love these small rooms. Such lovely windows and what a delightful view,' she said, pointing across to the commanding mass of Arthur's Seat.

Faro suppressed a smile. The rooms with their high ceilings could only be classed as small by comparison. 'Hardly what you're used to in a palace, miss.'

'I know. But it's all so charming. Palaces are hateful places to live in, I assure you. There is so little comfort, vast rooms with inadequate fires to heat them, miles and miles to walk every time one wants something that isn't there.' She clasped her hands delightedly. 'I would give anything to live in a little house like this.'

'Excuse me, miss — the kettle —'

When he returned, she was sitting close to the dead fire, her arms clasped tightly together.

Faro sighed. 'I'm afraid that's beyond redemption, miss. It is chilly in here.'

Politely she suppressed a shiver. 'Just a little.'

'It's warmer in the kitchen, miss, a good fire down there. Would you care —'

'I would indeed.' And seizing her bag, she followed him downstairs. There her admiration of his home now extended to Mrs Brook's domain. She looked around at shelves and cupboards as if she had never encountered a kitchen before, exclaiming with delight over gleaming brass saucepans and rows of china plates.

'You should see our kitchen in the castle. It's a terrible place, big and gloomy as a dungeon. Oh, do please — allow me —'

And Faro, rather relieved, handed her Mrs Brook's precious tea-caddy. Watching her he suddenly laughed out loud.

'What is so amusing?' she asked.

'You're better than I am at tea-making. Of course, I should have expected that in a lady-in-waiting. I suppose it's part of your duties.'

She smiled. 'Not really. It's usually brought in all prepared.' And as he took out Mrs Brook's cake: 'I'd love a slice of that —'

As she ate, Faro, having reassembled his thoughts, decided he must escort her back to Lethie Castle immediately, a double journey he could well do without. Her impulsive action was a nuisance and a waste of his time, but he could sympathize with the anxiety and boredom that had driven her to escape for the day.

The Lethies, he guessed, would by now have discovered her absence. Perhaps she did not realize in her sheltered life in Luxoria that in respectable society, ladies of gentle birth did not promenade the streets and shops of Edinburgh, even during the day, unescorted or without a maid in attendance. And despite the note she had left, Sir Terence and his wife would be frantic with anxiety when they realized she had gone off alone.

He sighed. Somehow on the way to Aberlethie he must tactfully get her to understand that he had no authority to set out for Balmoral Castle with her and make an impromptu visit to the Royal residence on the assumption that her mistress was already there.

If only he could believe that were true, what a happy man he would be.

He smiled at her, so pretty and gentle. And safe too when just a few hours ago, while she was promenading along Princes Street, he feared she might have been in grave danger. What an opportunity the hired assassin had missed there, he thought with a shudder.

He looked at the clock. 'There's a train back to Aberlethie in half an hour. We'll take that one.'

She allowed him to help her into her cape somewhat reluctantly. 'Oh, very well. I suppose I must go. But I've so enjoyed talking to you, Inspector, you have been very kind.'

As he picked up her bag she seized it back from him. 'I'll take that, thank you.'

He wondered what it contained that was so precious, deciding that it was remarkably heavy and solid too, for feminine fripperies. But rather admiring her independence, he said:

'You wait here in the hall, miss. I'll get a carriage.'

A few minutes later they were heading towards Waverley Station. Armed with their tickets, Faro led her towards the platform.

At the barrier, the guard shook his head. 'Not tonight, I'm afraid, sir.'

Faro pointed towards the waiting train.

'Aye, sir, and there it stays till morning. There's been a cloud burst, line is flooded past Musselburgh and there'll be no trains till it subsides.' The porter looked at the grey sky. 'If it stays fine, then you'll get away first thing tomorrow morning.'

Faro regarded Miss Fortescue anxiously as they walked back into the booking office.

'Don't worry, miss, we'll get you back somehow.'

But far from being worried or dismayed, Miss Fortescue laughed, obviously treating this new disaster as a huge joke. 'Here's a pretty pickle. Well, Inspector, how do you solve this one?'

'That's easy, miss. We take a carriage.'

'What an adventure.' She chuckled happily.

It was the kind of adventure Faro could well have done without when he saw that the usual line-up of hiring carriages was absent from outside the station. At last a solitary one appeared and Faro rushed forward.

'Where to, sir?' asked the coachman.

'Aberlethie, if you please.'

'Aberlethie, did ye say?' The man shook his head. 'Not tonight, sir. Just come from Musselburgh, that's as far as we can get. Roads are all under water. You and the missus'll need to wait till morning and take a train like sensible folk.'

And looking at Miss Fortescue's bag, presuming they had come off a train, he said: 'I can take you to a good hotel.'

'A hotel.' Miss Fortescue grasped his arm. 'Oh no, Inspector, I couldn't — I just couldn't,' she whispered.

'Why ever not, miss? There are some very comfortable establishments on Princes Street. Very respectable too.'

'I'm sure there are. It isn't that, I assure you. I'm just — scared.'

'Scared?'

'Yes. You see, I once stayed in a hotel and it took fire. So I can't.' She shook her head firmly. 'Not ever again.'

He wasn't sure that he wanted to let her out of his sight, aware that she might have been followed. 'I'll stay there too, if you wish. Take a room close to yours —'

'No — no — you're very kind. But not even if you were in the — the same room — I just — can't.'

'Are you wanting this carriage or not?' the coachman demanded.

If it was possible that she had been followed, then Faro could see dangers in the hotel idea. He now had to consider reluctantly the alternative that remained. And that was to keep her under his own roof where he could be sure she was safe till morning.

And as if she read his thoughts: 'Perhaps you have a spare room,' she whispered.

Chapter 14

The carriage set them down in Sheridan Place and as Faro opened his front door, Miss Fortescue sighed.

'I'm greatly obliged to you, Inspector.'

Faro led the way down to the kitchen. And deploring Mrs Brook's absence, he said: 'Take a seat by the fire and I'll see what I can do about a room for you.'

Where would he put her? He seldom set foot in the spare rooms and had no idea whether the housekeeper kept beds made up for unexpected guests. He soon discovered that was not the case. The rooms he entered were cold and desolate, beds stripped down to their mattresses.

So where were the sheets and blankets kept? He wasn't even sure he knew how to make a bed properly.

Then he remembered his daughters' room and throwing open the door, Mrs Brook's proud boast that it was always kept aired and in readiness for their next visit was evidently correct.

Miss Fortescue followed him upstairs and setting down her bag by the bed, she looked round delightedly at her surroundings.

'Thank you so much, Inspector. Yes, I'm sure I'll be most comfortable.'

'Let me know if there is anything you require, miss.'

A few minutes later she returned to the kitchen, where he was spreading the table with some of Mrs Brook's abundant provisions.

'Such a pretty room you've given me. Is it your sister's?'

'No, my two daughters occupy it when they come to stay during the school holidays.' He was ashamed at making those sadly infrequent visits sound so regular.

'They are not at school in Edinburgh?'

'No.' He explained to her that he was a widower and it was convenient for his daughters to stay with their grandmother in Orkney.

She was all sympathy. Very sweet, he decided, and a good listener. Splendid appetite, too. She obviously relished Mrs Brook's cooking and begged to be allowed to take over preparation of the meal. Far from being baffled by cavernous pantries and belligerent stoves, she found one of Mrs Brook's vast aprons and was soon in complete command of the domestic situation.

Faro looked on, laughing approvingly. 'I'm glad you came, miss.'

She shook her head, smiled. 'Not miss, please. Roma.'

'Roma,' he repeated. 'An unusual name.'

'My parents spent their honeymoon in Italy.'

As they enjoyed a pleasant and companionable meal together he found himself telling her not only his life story, but his problems at the Central

Office and even details of some of his most baffling cases. He found she had a surprising knowledge of the major governmental issues in Britain, as well as a keener understanding than he had ever aspired to, of the boiling-pot of European politics.

Miss Roma Fortescue, he guessed, belonged to the new breed of independent and enlightened women. And Faro was one man who didn't feel threatened by them. In many of his cases, he had learned to deal with women who were the equal of any man, and infinitely more ruthless. He had his own personal reasons, and carried some indelible scars, for regarding the fair sex not as the weaker, but in many instances, the stronger.

This one, he thought, was far too bright to be wasted in a stultifying existence as a mere lady-in-waiting to an impulsive headstrong Royal Duchess, with her talents limited to plying an embroidery needle, playing the piano-forte and playing up to her mistress's constant demand for entertainment.

Afterwards, when he tried to do so, he could never clearly remember details of their conversation, only her ready flashes of wit and humour.

As she cleared the table and carried the dishes to the sink, refusing his help, she sighed happily. 'This is my dream come true. I get so little chance to do this sort of thing. I am not even allowed to set foot in the kitchens.' She paused and looked at him solemnly. 'Shall I tell you what my favourite book is?'

'Please do,' he said, expecting some learned philosophical treatise.

'Promise you won't laugh.'

'I promise.'

'Mrs Beeton's *All About Cookery* book.' She looked at him suspiciously. 'You don't find that amusing?'

'On the contrary, I find it very worthy.'

She looked around and smiled. 'A kitchen, warm — and small. A cosy fire and a table full of baking materials. Half a dozen menus to prepare — that is my idea of bliss.'

'And a husband perhaps to appreciate your culinary efforts,' he added teasingly.

Her face darkened. 'Perhaps.' Then the shadow lifted and she regarded him intently, with a look that flattered him. 'Or a kind friend. That would do perfectly.'

Faro wondered why, past thirty, she was still unmarried. He suspected a sad love story, some hidden grief. Pretty, charming, attractive — were Luxorian men daunted by such qualities and by this clever Scotswoman? Scots? No. She wasn't really, he thought, she was quite foreign sometimes, in turns of phrase, a word sought after vainly — in the manner of British subjects who spend most of their lives in other countries and are more at home in another language.

He was delighted to find that Miss Fortescue was extremely well-read. She shared his own passion for Shakespeare's plays, her early years as companion to her English-educated Royal mistress had obviously served her well. He was agreeably surprised to hear that she also enjoyed Sir Walter Scott's novels.

'And we had all Mr Dickens' latest books sent out specially to Luxoria.'

Music too, Faro discovered, was something they shared. Mr Mendelssohn and Mr Liszt had been welcome visitors to Luxoria.

In no great hurry to bring the evening to a close, they talked and laughed together. Meanwhile the storm continued to rage outside, but they were oblivious of wind lashing the windows, of doors creaking in the gale.

At one stage, pouring more wine, Faro looked at his companion and saw her for the first time as a woman to be desired. He realized wistfully that this cosy domestic scene, this simple meal in a warm kitchen was one being repeated in houses all over Edinburgh.

How long had it been since he spent an evening at home with a woman he loved, he thought wistfully, his hand shaking a little as he picked up his wineglass? It had been so long since Lizzie died. His skirmishes into love had been transient, wounding, disastrous.

As Miss Fortescue looked at him he felt embarrassed by the pain in his eyes. Was she lonely too? Did this kitchen scene remind her of the years that were gone, of sad days and glad days and lost love.

Faro sighed. The Wagnerian storm outside with its lightning flashes and thunder-claps that shook the walls and guttered the lamps was all the passion this particular house would know tonight.

Midnight was past. Where had the hours gone? He wanted to call them all back again, to relive each minute, suddenly precious, each sentence, each burst of laughter in a perpetual motion of happy hours. Eternity should be such a night as this. Eternal bliss —

And now it was almost over. Miss Fortescue stood up, yawned. He regarded the dregs of his empty wineglass.

'Of course, you must be tired.'

She sighed. 'A little, yes. It has been such a day.'

He poured warm water into a ewer for her washing and took the candle off the table. 'I'll see you to your room.'

He followed her upstairs, opened the door of his daughters' room for her. Turning, she smiled. 'Such a lovely day. A tremendous adventure.'

'I'll bid you goodnight, miss. Sleep well.'

'You too, Inspector. And thank you once again.'

Here today, gone tomorrow a bird of passage, with plumage strange and rare. Only a fool would fall in love, Faro thought, closing the door on her.

His dreams were wild and strange, full of erotic images. The Crusader came from his tomb, stalking him across the years and thrusting the Luck of Lethie into his hands. It turned into a snake becoming part of his own body.

173

He was awake. It was that strange hour twixt wolf and dog when familiar shapes of furniture become gross and ghostly aliens of nightmare and all the world holds its breath.

Someone was shaking him.

'Wake up — please, wake up.'

It was Miss Fortescue.

'Someone — someone is trying to break into the house, she whispered. 'In the kitchen —'

Faro leaped out of bed and threw on his dressing-robe. An attempted break-in. There could be only one purpose. He felt sickened and confused by the knowledge that someone had followed Miss Fortescue and knew she was here. The assassin —

'You stay here,' he said, and ran lightly downstairs.

The kitchen was filled with grey uneasy dawn. But the door was still locked, bolted.

'They must have run away,' Miss Fortescue whispered. She was brave, he thought, she had followed him.

'What made you think — ?'

'I heard a noise. I was thirsty, too much wine, I suppose. You didn't leave me a carafe —'

Cutting short his apologies: 'My fault. I didn't ask. I came downstairs. And I saw a shadow — a man — at the window. Look —' She pointed.

He went to the window above the sink. A small pane of glass was broken. He opened the back door cautiously, walked the few steps to the window, saw the slivers of glass on the ground.

She watched him relocking the door.

174

'Well, you must have scared him off,' he said. 'I think you'd better go back to bed.'

'Are you sure he won't come back?' she said, pointing to the window.

'No. No one could climb in through that tiny space. I think we're safe enough now.'

She walked ahead of him up the stairs. She was wearing a light petticoat, prettily frilled with ribboned lace and he realized that she must have slept in it in the absence of a nightgown.

He opened her bedroom door. 'You'll be quite safe now.'

'But — how —'

He shook his head, gently closed the door on her protests and went back to his own bed.

There he lay awake, his hands behind his head, pondering the night's strange events. In a little while he dozed, and opening his eyes, he thought he dreamed again, for she stood at his bedside.

'I'm so frightened. And I'm so cold. I've never been so cold.'

She held out her hands. He smiled and pulled back the covers, taking her into his arms. She was as passionate as she was clever, as tender as she was sweet.

At last the storm rolled away, and the golden light of early morning sunlight touched the bed where they lay still entwined.

Faro sighed, looking at her sleeping face. Soon it would be all over. The wild sweetness of one stolen night about to be obliterated by another day when dreams are quenched by the solemnity of duty.

She stirred in his arms. He kissed her hair and left her.

When she came down to the kitchen where he was stirring up the embers of the fire, she looked towards the broken pane of glass.

'I can't believe it really happened,' she whispered.

'It didn't.'

'You mean — the break-in.'

'Exactly. It didn't happen. There never was a burglar.' He put an arm around her and laughed. 'So much trouble to come into my bed,' he whispered.

She understood. Laughing lightly, standing on tiptoe, she kissed him.

Chapter 15

Sergeant McQuinn arrived as they were leaving the house together. He managed to conceal well both his surprise and his curiosity at the presence of a young woman in Inspector Faro's hall at eight thirty in the morning.

Saluting smartly, for the lady's benefit, he said: 'Superintendent McIntosh's compliments, sir. He needs to see you urgently.'

'I was about to escort Miss Fortescue back to Aberlethie.'

McQuinn looked at Miss Fortescue. 'Perhaps I can do that for you, sir.' He pointed to the street. 'The carriage is there.'

McQuinn did not miss the lady's frantic look in Faro's direction nor how completely the Inspector chose to ignore it.

'You will be quite safe with Sergeant McQuinn, miss. Er — I'll call on you later.'

Bowing to her, he felt that he failed completely to convey the emotion concealed within those few words. She darted him a frantic look as McQuinn reached out a hand for her bag. But refusing to be parted from it, she allowed him to hand her into the carriage.

Again Faro wondered what shopping had been so precious or so heavy and, more important, where the money had come from. Obviously Lady Lethie had been generous with more than her wardrobe.

Helplessly he watched them go, lifting a hand in farewell, angry at McIntosh's ill-timed command and with a shaft of jealousy for the young Irishman.

Would McQuinn exert all his ready charm on Miss Fortescue, Faro thought, remembering how successful McQuinn was with the ladies? All ages too, even his own young daughter Rose had lost her heart to him.

But in another part of his mind, Faro was secretly relieved that McQuinn's arrival had been so opportune. No words of love had been spoken between Roma Fortescue and himself. They had been two lonely people hungry for comfort. Of greater embarrassment would have been an explanation of why she had felt it necessary to pretend there was a burglar lurking on the premises.

That failed to make any sense at all.

In the Central Office, he found Superintendent McIntosh pacing the floor anxiously.

'Where do you think you've been, Faro? I've been waiting for you here since eight o'clock.'

Faro did not feel up to explaining that his arrival had been delayed by Miss Fortescue's departure on the nine o'clock train for North Berwick. Superintendent McIntosh would doubtless have asked the question he was most anxious to avoid: What was she doing at his house and where had she spent the night?

'There's a couple of lads downstairs. Claim that the man you found in St Anthony's Chapel is their father. They're with Dr Cranley now. He wants you to talk to them.'

The downstairs room was stark and bare with whitewashed brick walls and a disagreeable smell. Used for the questioning of criminals, its intimidating atmosphere offered little by way of consolation in breaking bad news to bereaved relatives.

Constable Reid was in attendance and Dr Cranley indicated a seat at the table. As he sat down opposite the pair, the doctor said: 'This is Inspector Faro.'

Introductions were unnecessary, the Hogan brothers knew him well already. Their paths had crossed many times before, and as far as Faro could see the only thing they had in common with the dead man was ginger hair.

'. . . They have identified the body as that of their father, Joshua Hogan, aged fifty-five, who went missing from home two weeks ago. I have explained the circumstances of his discovery to them and they have made a statement . . .'

As Cranley spoke, Faro studied the two men. The elder, Joe, was a petty criminal, a fence for stolen goods, the younger, Willy, a pimp for their sister, a notorious prostitute. All three had at some time been involved in fraud cases.

'Have you any idea what caused your father's death?' Faro asked.

'Bad lungs, he had,' said Joe, who had appointed himself spokesman. 'He was fooling around, drunk as usual. Fell into the horse trough outside the World's End Tavern. Lads he was with were all larking about, didn't realize he was dead, took him home, put him to bed. Willy and me wasn't home — we was at the horse sales in Glasgow, so he lay for a week. When we got back lads was scared they'd be blamed, and to cut a long story out, they carted him up to St Anthony's, dumped him there.'

'Have you names and addresses of these lads?'

'They're on the paper there,' Hogan said smoothly. 'Constable wrote them down along with our statement. Gave my word no harm would come to them. Gave my hand on it.'

And I dare say you had a lot of money pressed into it, thought Faro grimly. He looked at Dr Cranley, whose expression said he didn't believe a word of it either.

'And here's Da's birth certificate, if you want it,' said Willy carelessly.

'What next?' Faro asked McIntosh after the pair of highly improbable grieving relatives had left.

'Not a great deal,' the Superintendent replied, glancing through their statements.

'Dammit, the man was murdered.'

'We can't prove it. You know that and so do I.'

'The Hogans are criminals —'

'And so are all their friends. They'll all swear blind that the brothers are speaking the truth.'

'I want to look further into it, sir. I'm not prepared to let it go at that.'

'You're wasting your time, Faro.'

'I've done that before and I'm prepared to do it again in the cause of justice.'

'Then try not to bring down a hornet's nest on our heads.'

'If it means bringing a murderer to justice, I'll even do that, sir.'

When McIntosh looked doubtful, Faro asked angrily:

'Look, you don't believe that story, do you, sir?'

'It's just daft enough to be true. The whole family is wild —'

'Extortionists, fraudsters —' Faro began heatedly.

'But always clever enough to evade arrest. There's money behind them.' The Superintendent shook his head. 'We all know that.'

'Stolen goods, smugglers, too. And no lack of alibis —'

'We haven't a hope in hell of finding who's backing them, Faro,' McIntosh interrupted impatiently.

'Why not?'

'He's not in our "Secret and Confidential" files, that's why. He could be a foreigner. Or a stranger — we have Highlanders, Irishmen, God knows all, passing through the warrens of the High Street

181

every day and lurking in the sewers of Worm-woodhall.'

'Then we should be looking for whoever is behind them, the man who pays them.'

'Indeed we should. He should be the subject of your most scrupulous investigations,' said McIntosh primly.

'And I'm starting right now, sir,' said Faro, picking up the statement that Dr Cranley had given him.

He spent the rest of the morning in the area of the High Street that the Hogans called home, known to the constables on the beat as the Thieves Kitchen.

Much to his surprise he found the first two men on the list readily enough. They were sitting smoking their clay pipes on their front doorstep. For once they were not in the least troubled by the arrival of a senior detective. They greeted him genially, ready and agreeably available to answer his questions.

Too readily available, even anxious to corroborate in exact detail the statement that the Hogan brothers had made, thought Faro grimly.

'Aye, we kenned the auld fella well, a demon for the drink he was, right enough. Ever since he left the sea, two months ago and arrived back in Edinburgh, nothing but trouble —'

Faro left with a warning that they could be charged with criminal activity. Concealing a dead man. They were not easily frightened by this threat of the law and Faro realized that it would be a waste of time talking to the other two youths on the list.

He walked down the street, conscious of their sniggers behind his back, knowing that for a couple of golden guineas they would have sworn that their grandmother was the Archbishop of Canterbury and their grandfather the Pope in Rome.

His way back to the Central Office took him past the head of Bowheads Wynd. He stopped and regarded it thoughtfully.

His cousin's observations had confirmed his own suspicions that the lad Sandy had been withholding vital information. A word with the lad might be all of use he was going to get out of an otherwise wasted morning.

He would take Leslie's sound advice, persuade Sandy Dunnock by gentle means and a lubrication of silver, or if that failed, something more forceful like a threat or two, to disclose in full the events of that fatal night.

It was not to be.

There was a small crowd gathered around the tall land where Sandy lived. With a sense of foreboding, Faro pushed his way through.

Two constables were already there bending over Sandy Dunnock, who lay with his arms outstretched to the sky. Unmarked except for the back of his head, mercifully hidden, and the angle of his neck.

He was dead.

'Capering about on the roof. Lost his footing,' Constable Boyd told Faro, as they prepared to carry Sandy's broken body up to the top floor.

Faro followed them inside, suddenly feeling old and sick. As they climbed the stairs, he asked Constable Boyd what had happened.

'I've already talked to his mother. She was sleeping. Heard nothing. In a bit of a state, as you can imagine. Neighbours are with her.'

Faro stopped, leaned against the cold stone wall. 'What was he doing on the roof?'

'Someone was chasing him. Escaping from the police, so the folk down there say.' Listening to Boyd's account, Faro had already substituted 'murderer' for 'police'. He had come too late and someone had effectively silenced for ever any dangerously revealing answers Sandy might have given to his questions.

The accident or murder of Sandy made Faro angrier than he had been so far, and with anger came determination to solve the case. He would no longer tread gently or discreetly either, for fear of distressing any royalty involved. Death was the same in the end whether you were a duchess or an Edinburgh pickpocket.

Boyd's account ended: 'Folk below saw it all. One of Sandy's cronies said he was running away from a tall man, looked like an old soldier. Had a scarred face. They'd seen him about —'

Even as Faro returned to the street below aware that the description fitted Sergeant Batey, Leslie Godwin was hurrying to meet him.

The few of the small crowd who had not discreetly vanished at the sight of the police, shouted curses at the tall sergeant walking at his master's side. A few of the bolder ones threw stones.

And that was all the confirmation Faro needed before Leslie said a word.

'I know why you're here, Jeremy. And I'm desperately sorry about the accident. Should never have happened. I saw the lad Sandy. He recognized me and Batey here. When I called that I wanted a word with him — I just wanted to tell him that you had money to give him, dammit, but I never got a chance. He wouldn't listen, thought we had it in for him because of the pickpocket business. He took to his heels, Batey in pursuit — you know the rest. God, I can't tell you how awful I feel. I blame myself —'

'You weren't to blame for his bad conscience,' said Faro in a poor attempt at consolation.

'Has the lad any family?' his cousin asked.

'A mother and siblings.'

'Right,' said Leslie, taking out a purse from his pocket and weighing it in his hand. 'I shall go and see them. I know it won't replace the lad, but it's the best I can do.'

As they turned towards the house, Faro said to Constable Boyd: 'You'd better accompany Mr Godwin. Might be trouble.'

'Thank you, Jeremy. Oh God, what an infernally sad business. If there's one thing I never get used to it's talking to bereaved relatives.' He sighed. 'You stay here, Batey,' he shouted over

185

his shoulder to the sergeant.

And looking very unhappy indeed, Leslie started up the stone stairs with Constable Boyd.

Faro, left alone with Batey, said: 'Tell me exactly what happened, if you please.'

Batey shrugged. For a moment Faro thought he was going to ignore the question. 'Come on, man, I need to know. You're a witness to a fatal accident.'

'Told the constable. Ask the people who saw it,' Batey said sullenly. 'They'll tell you what you want to know.' And unrepentant, he grinned, turned on his heel and walked away with such an insolent swagger that Faro had a sudden desire for violence.

Staring after him, clenching his fists, he was still shaking with impotent rage when Constable Boyd reappeared.

'Mr Godwin is with the lad's mother now. She wouldn't let me in, started screaming abuse at the sight of this —' he added, pointing to his uniform.

And Faro knew he could no longer avoid playing his part in this sad drama by visiting Mrs Dunnock, although God only knew what kind of comfort and consolation he could offer for the loss of her eldest bairn, doubtless the breadwinner in the household.

The words he rehearsed as he climbed the stairs sounded like cold sympathy, sentiments that always stuck in his throat.

The door was slightly ajar, and although the

dreadful smell he had first encountered had moderated somewhat, the sound of weeping deterred him.

Leslie emerged and shook his head, and taking Faro's arm he led him away. 'Don't advise it, Jeremy. Not just now. Leave it for a while. I've done all I can.'

As they walked down the stairs, Mrs Dunnock appeared on the landing above them, her tear-stained face pale and strained, staring over the iron railing.

'Don't you bring your polis back here. Not never,' she shouted to Faro. 'We don't want your sort here. Bastards,' she screamed, and shook a fist so violently that the bangle she wore fell off and rolled down the stairs, landing at Leslie's feet.

Snatching it up he threw it back to her. With a final curse, she ran inside and banged the door shut.

'Poor woman,' said Leslie. 'At least she has a crowd of bairns and relations to help her through it all —'

'That bracelet,' said Faro. 'It looked quite valuable.'

'Quite a contrast to the rest of her.' Leslie nodded. 'I was thinking the very same thing. Doubtless booty from one of young Sandy's forays into crime.' And halting, he asked: 'What am I going to do about Batey?'

'I can't answer that question, Leslie.'

His cousin sighed. 'I don't know what to do, really I don't. You see, he believed he was helping me. When that happens, all other thoughts go to the wind. I suppose you've realized the poor creature is quite devoted to me. And a bit simple.'

Simple wasn't quite the word Faro had in mind for the unpleasant sergeant. Evil would have fitted his image much better.

'Head wound. Tortured too. I feel responsible for him. I really do. And he would lay down his life for me. Did once. You can't repay those debts of loyalty.' He paused. 'I gather your enquiries are still in the doldrums.'

'And likely to remain there,' Faro answered shortly. Declining his cousin's sympathy and cheerful suggestion that they sink their sorrows over a dram together, he excused himself.

He didn't feel sociable. He needed to think, and as he walked towards the High Street through the market booths, he found himself again considering the significance of recent events.

All around him stall-holders bawled their wares. Food and rags were the main sales. He hardly glanced at them.

And then he saw it hanging at the front of a rag stall, in the place of honour. A handsome travelling cloak, violet wool with a velvet collar.

Could it be — ?

To his question 'How much?', he was told one guinea.

Such a high price was unusual, pennies were the usual currency on rag stalls, and this high price was doubtless the reason why it had remained unsold.

'Have you had it long?'

The stall-keeper, suspecting this well-dressed customer was a gentleman and a prospective buyer, eyed him keenly as he examined the garment. And when Faro repeated the question:

'A wee while, ye ken. Too guid for the folk round here. They're only wantin' rags.'

'Where did you come by such a handsome garment, may I ask?'

The stall-keeper didn't like the question. He avoided Faro's eyes, murmured cautiously, 'Came from somewhere, big house over Glasgow way.' Then afraid that he might be losing his best sale of the day, he added anxiously: 'Your lady wife would look grand in it, so she would —'

A piercing whistle interrupted him. He froze and stared at Faro, who knew the signal had been given. The booth-holders had recognized the presence of a detective in their midst. That spelt trouble and his identity had been speedily declared.

'I'll take it,' said Faro, and thrusting the money into the man's hand, he grabbed the cloak even as the stall-holder attempted to snatch it back again.

'You're right,' he said. 'My wife will be delighted.'

As he walked away with it over his arm, he wondered how Miss Fortescue would react to seeing what he was certain sure had been the cloak her mistress was wearing on the night she disappeared.

Chapter 16

Faro abandoned his first inclination to go straight out to Aberlethie. For one thing, he felt self-conscious about travelling on the North Berwick train with a woman's cloak over his arm. Doubtless there would be some suitable receptacle in Mrs Brook's capacious cupboard.

And thoughts of Mrs Brook reminded him of a more urgent reason for a return to Sheridan Place. In his hurry to leave that morning he had omitted to clear up the broken glass from outside the window.

There was a glazier in the Pleasance and he hoped that the repair could be carried out before the housekeeper returned.

The glazier was reassuring, but when Faro opened his front door he discovered that the conscientious Mrs Brook had been unable to stay away. He found her with Vince outside the kitchen door, staring in consternation at the damaged window.

'I was just saying to Dr Vince here that this sort of thing never happened before when I was in the house,' said Mrs Brook in outraged tones. 'Looks like someone trying to break in, sir —'

'I know about it, Mrs Brook,' Faro interrupted. 'No harm done. It was an accident.'

She regarded him curiously. 'Oh, was it, sir?' she asked, obviously expecting some explanation — but that he wasn't prepared to supply. 'I was just about to clear it up when Dr Vince said you had better see it first.'

'You may clear it now, Mrs Brook, if you please. The glazier will come later today.'

'Very well, sir. We wouldn't want to attract burglars, would we now?'

Faro smiled. 'I should think the size of the windowpanes would deter any but a very tiny criminal. You might have more success with your admirable floor polish,' he added pointedly.

Mrs Brook didn't find that amusing. 'First thing I did was get Dr Vince to go through the house with me, make sure all was in order.'

'And was it?'

She exchanged a look with Vince. 'Oh yes, sir.'

Vince had remained silent throughout this conversation. He followed Faro upstairs. Pausing, he looked at the violet cloak on the hallstand.

'That's new, Stepfather,' he said lightly. 'Hardly your colour, is it?' he added.

'I have quite a lot to tell you,' said Faro.

'I thought you might have,' said Vince, and his mocking tone as he led the way into his consulting rooms made Faro distinctly uneasy.

Faro quickly outlined the events of the previous day, the finding of the body at St Anthony's Chapel, and his subsequent interview with the Hogan family, ending with the death of the lad Sandy.

191

Vince listened carefully. 'So you think this man they claimed to be the Hogan parent could be the missing coachman?'

'The timing of his disappearance certainly fits. He could have been hired on that particular occasion. And provided that the pounds Scots offered were tempting enough, he would refrain from asking too many questions.'

'In his case, that was a pity, since once his job was completed, he was then disposed of.'

'True. And I suspect that all they had in common was the colour of their hair,' said Faro. 'But I expect they were paid handsomely to tell the story about him being their drunken old father, drowned in a horse trough.'

'But why keep the body? Why didn't they dump both of them?'

'Don't you see, lad? One murder could be passed off as a heart attack, but it would have been exceedingly difficult with a drowned man to make it look as if both had died of natural causes after taking shelter in the West Bow. Even the Wizard's House couldn't be guaranteed to rise to those dizzy heights of imagination.'

Vince thought for a moment. 'So someone concealed him — for a price — until the woman's body had been neatly disposed of and there would be no connection between the two deaths.'

'Exactly — But how and, more important, where?' When Vince didn't reply, he added: 'The answer to both queries is — for a handsome price to make the risk worth while. And if we can find out who paid the Hogans, we will be well on the way to solving both murders.'

'So you think Sandy knew something.'

'I do, indeed. It was a very unfortunate co-incidence that his guilty conscience regarding petty thefts made him run away from Batey —'

Vince shivered. 'I'd have done the same, even without a bad conscience, if that face had been pursuing me —'

Faro sighed. 'I'm afraid this is one mystery I'm never going to solve, Vince. There are too many threads, weaving in and out and leading nowhere. And the worst isn't over yet, I'm convinced of that. If my suspicions are correct, the Queen will have to be told, God knows how she will take it — or Superintendent McIntosh when he knows the truth. I'll probably be out of a job, and Dr Cranley, too. What a scandal. We'll be lucky if we don't spend the rest of our lives locked up.'

'Come now, Stepfather. It isn't like you to give in so easily. You're a fighter, remember?' And with a shrewd glance, he added softly: 'Your emotions are too involved with this one.'

Emotions. Yes, Vince was right.

'You had something more you were going to tell me, I believe,' said Vince gently.

'Had I?'

'I think so. Such as who was sleeping in your daughters' bed last night.'

Damn, thought Faro. Why hadn't she made up her bed or, more to the point, why hadn't he checked it to make sure? Another blunder like leaving the broken glass outside.

He sighed. 'I gave a benighted traveller shelter. You saw what the weather was like.'

Vince ignored that. 'And —' he prompted.

'What do you mean — and?' Faro tried to sound outraged, hoping his tone would discourage any further discussion.

'I want to know more about this stranger. Was this benighted traveller trying to escape? Was there a fight? Is that why the window was broken?'

'Of course not. It could have been anything, a flying roof-tile during the storm, I expect.' Faro had already decided on this as a promising explanation.

'Come now, Stepfather. You and I both know better than that. This window was broken from the inside, otherwise the glass would have been on the sill not in the garden. What was going on?'

At his stepfather's expressionless face, he asked gently, 'Who are you trying to protect?'

When Faro looked away, Vince murmured: 'A lady's honour, perhaps.' And when he didn't answer. 'I suspect there is a lady involved. I'm as gallant as the next man, so you'd better tell all. I might even be able to help.'

Faro remembered ominously that the last person who had suggested he might be able to help had been his cousin Leslie and that had ended in Sandy's death. Faro felt he would never quite cease to blame himself in some measure for the lad's tragic end.

'Miss Fortescue stayed here last night —'

And Faro told him the whole story, omitting that after coming to his bed to report a suspected burglar, she had stayed there too.

'What extraordinary behaviour,' said Vince. 'Why on earth should she do such a thing? Unless —' He paused.

'Unless what — ?'

'It is possible that the lady wanted some attention from you and by pretending — of course, it is a ridiculous suggestion.'

That wounded Faro into saying: 'I don't find it in the least ridiculous.' Too late, he saw that he had fallen neatly into the trap.

Vince's smile was triumphant. 'Ah!'

'Oh, very well. She was scared, so she said. She spent the rest of the night with me.'

Vince nodded, he wasn't taken aback as Faro thought he might be. 'So what happens next?'

'How the devil do I know!'

'Stepfather — don't explode — I'm trying to help, remember. All I want to know for your own good, is — are you in love with this Miss Fortescue?'

'I haven't had time to think about it,' said Faro shortly.

'Then I suggest you take time to do just that.' When Faro looked hard at him, Vince continued: 'Sounds rather as if she might be a suitable wife for you, if she could be persuaded to leave the warmer climate of Luxoria —'

Faro laughed. 'This is incredible. For once, the situation is reversed and I find myself having to listen to the sort of advice I am usually giving to you.'

'Don't change the subject, if you please,' said Vince sternly. 'Are you contemplating asking her to be your wife?'

'No,' said Faro shortly.

'And why not? In the circumstances it would seem appropriate. Making an honest woman — and so forth —'

'According to convention, Vince, but then I have never been a slave to convention and I'm too old to start now.'

'You could try.'

Faro shook his head. 'I'm not in the least sure that Roma — Miss Fortescue — is bound by convention either. She seems as impulsive as her Royal mistress. And talking of that, do you honestly see an ex-Royal lady-in-waiting settling down in Sheridan Place and running a policeman's household?'

'You're not a policeman, you're a very senior detective, and not at all bad-looking, come to that. Yes, Stepfather.' Vince considered him thoughtfully. 'Even a quite conventional young woman might just leap at the prospect.'

'Rubbish. How could I support her in the luxury she has been used to in the household of Luxorian royalty?'

'Oh, do stop being such a snob, Stepfather.

Greater social leaps have been taken — and are being taken — every day. And I am assured by those who know that love is a bridge.'

'Love.' Faro shook his head sadly. 'I'm afraid I haven't got to that yet, Vince. I'm still bewildered by the whole thing, by a situation over which I seemed to have no control. All I can say is that I'm just damned sorry that it happened —'

'Then why didn't you send her packing before it began?'

Faro shivered. 'Because there was something wrong —'

'Wrong? How?'

'The whole night was odd, out of time, somehow — enchanted. Oh, I can't explain —'

'Can't you? Well, I can. It's happened to me many times,' said Vince. 'It's called infatuation, Stepfather. And I am very experienced in that particular field — as well you know,' he added bitterly.

'I've also fancied myself in love, Vince, but truly, I have never felt — well, taken over. I've always turned my face against magic, don't believe in it.'

Ignoring his stepson's cynical expression of disbelief, Faro continued: 'And yet last night, it was as if there was some other force here in this house. I even dreamed of the Luck of Lethie —'

'The famous fertility symbol.' Vince frowned. 'I hope not. What if she has a child —'

'Oh, don't be so damned ridiculous, Vince. I

dreamed of the Crusader alive, leaving his tomb. It was all so vivid.'

Vince's expression said that he was unimpressed and Faro went on hastily, 'Look, I neither want nor do I expect does she want, any lasting relationship. Not even a transient one, for that matter. There are too many mysteries surrounding that lady and her mistress.'

'Dangerous waters, I'd say,' Vince agreed. 'Best steer clear of them.'

Faro sighed. 'And talking of dangerous waters and the advisability of discretion, Cousin Leslie brought up the subject of our missing Duchess.' He stopped, reluctant to accuse Vince of betraying his trust.

But Vince merely smiled. 'Did he indeed?' What was he on about? 'I didn't realize you had confided in him?' He sounded surprised.

'I hadn't. But apparently you had,' Faro said angrily.

Vince's mouth dropped open and Faro cut short his protests.

'I gather you had rather a lot to drink and, well — in absolute confidence to a relative, of course — you let slip the whole damned business of the Royal disappearance.'

'I did WHAT?' Vince shook his head. 'I swear to you, Stepfather, I never mentioned it. I wouldn't, would I, for heaven's sake.'

'Not in the normal scheme of things, lad, but you know as well as I do what you're like when you have taken drink. Throw all your cares away and all discretion to the winds. You've never over-come your student recklessness —'

'Wait a minute. My own secrets, I grant you that. I can't be guaranteed to keep them. But not confidences relating to your criminals — or my patients. Such are sacrosanct.'

'Well, someone told him —'

'Honestly, Stepfather. I didn't. You must believe me. I never said a word —'

'Not that you remember, anyway,' said Faro coldly.

And Vince's further protests were cut short as the front doorbell rang and Mrs Brook admitted the doctor's first patient of the day.

Chapter 17

Hurt and angry at Vince's lack of discretion, Faro gathered his notes on the case which he would read on the train to Aberlethie.

As he glanced through them, there was something at the back of his mind, a significant fact or comment that had failed to register when he had heard it. Of the utmost importance, he felt this was the vital clue that still eluded him and held the solution of the mystery.

He sat down. The morning train to North Berwick was forgotten as in his precise neat handwriting he added to his notes an account of the death of Sandy Dunnock and his purchase of the violet cloak —

As he wrote, the scene came vividly before him —

The jewellery Miss Fortescue had told him that her mistress was wearing on that fatal night. He drew out the list, checked the items again.

'A gold chain with its eight-sided cross —' The same chain which he suspected was the one he had recovered from the Wizard's House lay in the open drawer beside him.

'A gold bracelet with a snake's head and ruby eyes —'

He threw down the pen with an exclamation

of triumph. For he knew where he had seen the bracelet. On Mrs Dunnock's wrist as she leaned over the stairhead in Bowheads Wynd, brandishing a fist at Leslie and himself, screaming abuse —

He saw it again slipping from her arm, falling at their feet. Saw Leslie throw it back to her —

The violet cloak, the visit to Aberlethie could wait. They were suddenly of minor importance compared to a visit to Bowheads Wynd and a confrontation with Sandy's mother.

It was not an interview Faro looked forward to as he climbed the odorous stairs. The door was opened a couple of inches and one of the Dunnock children peered out.

From inside, a shout: 'Who is it?'

'A man — I dinna ken him.'

'Tell him yer ma's no weel.'

Faro pushed his way in. 'I must talk to her.'

The room was crowded with mourners and Faro hated intruding on the woman's grief. Sandy had been confined. He lay on a trestle-table at one end of the room, his countenance pale and angelic in the face of death.

As Faro removed his hat and stared down at the lad, had he been able to lay hands on Batey at that moment, he would have dragged him here, forced him to look at this pathetic sight. Surely even his cold heart would have felt remorse for this sad waste of a young life.

Pushing his way through the neighbours, he observed that there was food and drink in plenty at this wake. Those he encountered knew who he was. They stepped aside hastily, averting their heads as if to avoid recognition or the touch of his shadow. He was unpleasantly aware of murmurs and hostile stares, of fists shaken after him.

Mrs Dunnock regarded him dully. 'What do ye want wi' us now? Have ye no' done enough?'

'I'm sorry, Mrs Dunnock. I bitterly regret what happened, but my men weren't responsible for your lad's death. You ken that fine well. The man chasing your lad had naught to do with us.'

Watching her closely he opened the bag, took out the violet cloak. He had the satisfaction of seeing recognition — and fear — as he asked:

'Is this yours?'

'Mine? Chance would be a grand thing.' She laughed harshly. 'I didn't steal it either if that's what you're getting at. I had nothing to do with that.'

That was all Faro needed to know. She had confirmed his suspicions of some connection between Sandy's family and their cronies regarding the disposal of the dead woman's garments. They had guessed their resale value and without too many scruples, had removed them and substituted a beggar's ragged gown.

He guessed that whatever had happened, her clothes had not suffered from immersion in the water as had Roma Fortescue's. It fitted neatly into the pattern that, terrified, she had died of a heart attack.

He held up the cape again to let Mrs Dunnock

have a good look. 'Did Sandy find it, then?' he asked gently.

In answer she turned her face away. 'I dinna ken — I dinna ken anything about it.'

Faro nodded. 'Thanks for your help. I am grateful.' As she gave him a look of surprise, he leaned forward and took her wrist as if to shake her by the hand. A quick look confirmed that the bracelet with its snake's head was no longer there.

'That bonny bangle you were wearing,' he said lightly, 'have you lost it?'

The fleeting panic in her eyes was swiftly replaced by mockery. 'Oh, is this what you mean?' And from her apron pocket she took a large brass curtain ring, the kind gypsies in the Lawnmarket sold for ten a penny.

Faro shook his head. 'No. The one with a snake's head.'

Avoiding his eyes, she said calmly, 'This is the only bangle I've ever had. The only kind the likes of me could afford.'

So she knew the value of the other one, Faro thought, as she continued: 'Your eyes must be going bad, mister, with staring into other folk's business.'

'Is this man bothering you, Meg?' The Hogan brothers came over. 'Get going, Inspector, there's nothing for you here. Leave the poor soul to mourn her lad.'

Faro left with the dubious satisfaction of knowing that Mrs Dunnock had lied. She had recognized the cloak and had been told to get rid of the bracelet.

The Hogans were certainly involved. They would have helped with the sale of the bracelet and the proceeds would have bought the abundant food and drink littering the table. Whoever was behind that sale, Faro thought grimly, was responsible for both deaths — of the woman in the West Bow and the drowned man in St Anthony's Chapel.

There seemed little point in making a special journey with the cloak for Miss Fortescue's further identification. That could wait, he decided as he returned to the Central Office.

McQuinn was walking up the front steps.

'Trains all back to normal, sir. Delivered the young lady right to the castle door. She suggested I leave her at the Aberlethie halt to make her own way across the grounds, but I insisted on escorting her.'

His glance was enigmatic, then he grinned. 'Much against her will, I fear. That's a very strong and independent lady — benighted in Edinburgh — all on her own too,' he added, shaking his head.

'Don't I know it. I had to give her a night's lodging.' Faro hoped he made it sound casual and unconcerned enough to convince his sergeant. 'How did Sir Terence and his lady react to her reappearance?'

McQuinn shrugged. 'They're very good at concealing their feelings, that class of people. Give nothing away, but Lady Lethie seemed uncommon relieved to see her. Quite pink she went. However, his lordship had more pressing problems than Miss Fortescue's return.'

'What kind of problems?'

'Well, as I was walking the young lady towards the house, one of the servants came rushing out followed by Mrs Hall, the housekeeper. She was very excited and agitated. She'd seen us coming down the drive from the kitchen window, "You got here fast, officer," says she. She'd recognized the uniform and thought I was there about the burglary.'

'Burglary? What burglary?' Faro demanded.

'Seems that one of the family treasures had been stolen.' He took out his notebook and read. 'The Luck of Lethie, they call it. Very old and very valuable. According to Mrs Hall, it was in its usual place a couple of nights ago when she checked that the windows were secure before going to bed. But the next morning, when she went in to see if the fires had been laid for the laird's return, the cabinet containing the Luck was empty.

'Naturally she gave the alarm and told the local constable — I've talked to him, sir, he confirms all this. Mrs Hall was in a proper panic, wondering what his lordship would say when he got back this morning. Wringing her hands, she was, usual story. They'd hold her responsible for what happened in their absence. Like as not lose her situation, be packed off without a reference.'

Faro's thoughtful expression indicated that he was well ahead, reconstructing the scene with quite a different explanation.

It was so simple, he should have known immediately. 'How did Miss Fortescue take all this? Was she scared?' he asked.

'Not a bit of it. Didn't seem to find it particularly interesting. Just dashed into the house and left us.'

'Ah,' sighed Faro happily, as McQuinn continued:

'I took the usual statements from the staff, sir. This had to be an inside job, there was no sign of forced entrance, doors and windows securely locked. I was assuring Mrs Hall that no one could blame her in such circumstances when his lordship appeared in a great hurry. Said it was all a mistake, that the Luck hadn't been stolen at all.'

'Indeed!'

'Rum business, sir, if you ask me. His lordship then went on to say it was back in its usual place, would I care to look? Right enough, it was there in the cabinet. His lordship then explained that he had had it removed for cleaning, and had completely forgotten to tell Mrs Hall. He was most apologetic for wasting our time.'

McQuinn stopped, frowned. 'You know sir, I didn't believe a word of it.' He paused. 'He was protecting someone — I just got that feeling. Do I proceed with this one, sir?'

'No need. We'll take his lordship's word for it.'

Faro didn't need to go to Lethie Castle to find the answer to the Luck of Lethie's miraculous reappearance.

He knew where it had been and who had taken it. All he needed to know was why.

A lot of light was suddenly being shed on the mystery. The only complication was that one particular facet which now concerned him personally was becoming darker and more sinister than ever.

As he was making some notes in his office, the door opened to admit Superintendent Mc-Intosh.

'Where do you think you've been, Faro? I've been waiting for you for hours.' He flourished a paper, effectively cutting short any of Faro's explanations.

'Never mind about that. You have a special assignment here, Faro. Direct from the PM. You're to take Miss Roma Fortescue, at present residing at Lethie Castle, to an assignation in Perth — to be presented to the Queen —' Pausing, he read, 'At Errol Towers, home of Her Majesty's equerry, Sir Piers Strathaird —'

'Why Perth?' Faro interrupted. 'Why can't she come to Holyrood?'

McIntosh stared at him angrily. 'I wasn't aware that we had any rights in deciding Her Majesty's movements about the country. It's one of her favourite jaunts, a decent distance from Balmoral, less than a day's ride.'

'I was thinking of security, sir,' said Faro.

'Oh, she knows what she's doing. Besides, what happens in Perth isn't the business of the Edinburgh City Police, Faro. I expect they have it all tied up nicely. Can't teach them their business, can we?'

McIntosh's grin suggested relief, a complete absence of the anxiety that generally added ten years to his age and decreased his life expectancy by a similar amount each time his sovereign set foot in Edinburgh.

'Seems the Grand Duchess of Luxoria is at present with Her Majesty at Balmoral.' He stared at the paper again. 'Naturally wants her lady-in-waiting —'

Faro stared at the Superintendent. 'The Grand Duchess is with the Queen? At Balmoral?'

McIntosh nodded. 'That's what it says. Here, read it for yourself.'

Faro stared at the letter written on the familiar personal notepaper of the Prime Minister. He had seen it many times and while it usually spelt trouble for him, the signature was undoubtedly Mr Gladstone's.

'The Grand Duchess wishes to be reunited with her lady-in-waiting Miss Roma Fortescue at the earliest.'

'How did the Grand Duchess get to Balmoral, sir?'

McIntosh shrugged. 'How the deuce do I know?'

'Well, aren't you curious, sir? She was reported as missing,' Faro reminded him. 'The last we heard of her was in an overturned carriage on the road from North Berwick from which she apparently vanished without trace.'

'Presumably someone assisted her.'

'They did indeed,' said Faro grimly. 'But who?'

'Don't ask me. She has a tongue in her head.' He gave Faro an arch look and shook his head sadly. 'I'm surprised at you not being sharper on to this one, Faro,' he said in the manner of one wise after the event. Tapping the side of his nose, he winked broadly. 'A secret assignation. Get the drift? One she was so canny about, she wasn't even taking her lady-in-waiting into her confidence.'

Pausing, he regarded Faro triumphantly. 'A man, Faro,' he said heavily. 'There's undoubtedly a man in this somewhere. I decided that right at the beginning,' he added carelessly. 'Knowing the circumstances of her unhappy marriage — and various rumours — it's quite obvious that this whole disappearance was a ruse, prearranged very carefully to get her and this man together.'

Faro sat back in his chair. Not for the first time, he wondered what kind of literature the Superintendent read in his leisure time. Here he was talking like a lady's novel and providing a rather superficial and improbable, but highly romantic, solution for a sinister disappearance.

Bewilderment was followed by relief. Although Faro couldn't yet believe that he had been wrong all the way along the line and that the man in St Anthony's Chapel and the beggar-woman in the West Bow were purely coincidental and unrelated deaths.

The Grand Duchess, who he thought had died in mysterious and inexplicable circumstances, her body disposed of by medical students, was not only alive and well, but sitting happily with her Royal godmother in Balmoral Castle.

And Faro was suddenly angry. 'They might have kept us informed, sir. We've been wasting time searching for a missing duchess, thinking the worst —'

McIntosh cut short this tide of justifiable resentment. 'Ours not to reason why, Inspector,' he said smoothly. 'The ways of royalty are not for us to question. Ours but to obey their command, however unreasonable it seems —'

'What about the woman in the West Bow — ?' Faro began.

McIntosh held up his hand, regarding him as if he had taken leave of his senses. 'A beggar-woman, Faro,' he emphasized. 'Are you seriously suggesting — ? Good Lord, what absolute nonsense.' And with a barking laugh of derision. 'How could you ever have entertained such a notion for one moment?'

McIntosh wagged a finger in Faro's face. He smiled, a happy man from whose shoulders all responsibility had been removed.

'After all, Her Majesty hasn't been in the best of health. Perthshire seems a suitable halfway meeting place. She and the late Prince Consort enjoyed many happy days at Errol Towers, you will doubtless recall. It no doubt has sentimental connections for their god-daughter too, more pleasantly informal than Holyrood. And takes far less heating.'

Pausing, he regarded Faro's sober expression. 'Come along, man. You should be glad, too, far less work involved for you.' And producing a map, he unrolled it carefully. 'Here, see. And as the railway goes right across a corner of the estate, there is a halt.'

This arrangement had become popular as well as desirable since the increase in train travel had opened up the length and breadth of Scotland. Now landowners were eager and most agreeable to allow this arrangement of a special halt, in return for permission to take the railway line directly across their estates, thus saving the cost of many extra miles of track. A new era had begun, hitherto undreamed of, offering travel from their very back doors, so to speak, instead of the slow, tortuous travel by carriage over often unmade roads with attendant inconvenience and discomfort.

'I don't need to tell you that you are to go alone, make this look as informal as possible. Travel by train as a couple can be done very discreetly. Besides, it is safer that way than by carriage.'

Faro looked at him quickly. 'You are suggesting by "safer" that some attempt might be made to stop Miss Fortescue joining her mistress?'

'Not at all,' was the smooth response. 'Merely in accordance with the desire of Her Majesty and the Grand Duchess for complete informality.'

McIntosh considered Faro's sombre expression. 'Come along, you are showing too much imagination.'

But it seemed that the Superintendent's laugh had a hollow sound and Faro could not shake off a sense of looming disaster.

The word 'safer' continued to haunt him and he left an urgent message for McQuinn on his way out of the office before returning briefly to Sheridan Place to thrust toilet articles, nightshirt and change of linen into a travelling bag.

As he closed his front door, he would have been happier with a more plausible explanation than the romantic supposition provided by Superintendent McIntosh of how the Grand Duchess of Luxoria had escaped presumably quite unhurt from an overturned carriage approaching Edinburgh one stormy night on the North Berwick road.

And, more important, what kind of woman was this, who would disappear with her lover without a second thought to the fate of a coachman as well as her closest friend and companion, leaving one to drown and the other to succumb to dying of fright?

If McIntosh were wrong, and Faro was certain that there was no lover involved, it was even more baffling. The Duchess had to have an accomplice, otherwise how had she got herself, a lone woman from a foreign country, with no experience of travel in Scotland, to the remote Royal residence of Balmoral Castle, two hundred miles away in Aberdeenshire? To complete such a journey, to arrive safely and thereupon to have access, unchallenged, to the Royal drawing-room would have presented a daunting prospect for any British national. For a foreign duchess who was used to having all arrangements planned in elaborate detail, to make such a journey unaided was beyond belief.

Beyond belief. Faro sighed, for that summed it up exactly. And instead of becoming clearer, the whole bizarre situation aroused every instinct for caution. In his vast experience of intrigue and crime, the pointers indicated a great deal of misinformation still to be unravelled. The signs also suggested that he was running out of time. He had better discover the truth quickly.

If he wished to stay healthy — and alive.

Chapter 18

Faro met Vince on the doorstep.

'Good! I left a note for you. I haven't much time, lad. A train to catch —' And drawing Vince inside he told him of the Queen's letter and his growing suspicions. This time he omitted nothing.

'But this is incredible. It can't be —' Vince protested.

'It is, I assure you. At the same time and with so much at stake, I'd give anything in the world to be proved wrong,' he added sadly.

Vince looked at him. 'You're going to need some help. And I'm committed to our damned Perth golf tournament.'

'You can't let down the team, lad.'

Faro listened carefully as Vince outlined his arrangements.

'At least we'll be heading in the same direction.'

'Damn the golf, Stepfather. Lives are at stake. Actually, it will fit in very well if I appear to be going there — I'll think of some last-minute excuse. In fact, I have a plan —'

Faro listened and shook his head. 'I don't want you involved in this,' he protested. 'I only want you to be in full possession of the facts — you know where to find them in my study — in case,' he added grimly, 'anything goes wrong —'

As he left the train at Aberlethie halt and walked through the grounds to Lethie Castle, Faro reflected on that fleeting interview with Vince, when he had had little time to do more than confide his suspicions. What if they were wrong and he had set in motion a tide of what was merely supposition?

He was shown into the drawing-room, where the Lethies appeared to be expecting him. Miss Fortescue was nowhere to be seen. He was glad of her absence so that he could test carefully the reactions of Sir Terence to the Prime Minister's summons.

When he produced the letter the Lethies could not conceal their relief. No one could blame them for being glad that someone was going to take the responsibility of their visitor off their hands. No matter how welcoming they had been, her presence would be an embarrassment as they prepared to depart for France.

As Lady Lethie rang the bell and a maid was sent for Miss Fortescue, Faro said:

'I understand your housekeeper had quite a scare. Thought there had been a burglary.'

'Burglary?' Sir Terence, still preoccupied with the contents of the letter Faro had produced, looked at him blankly. Then as realization dawned, he laughed. 'Oh, the Luck of Lethie, you mean. All a mistake, as your sergeant has no doubt told you. Come with me.'

Sir Terence led the way across the hall to the

library, eager to show Faro that all was well. There on the wall in its glass cabinet was the Luck of Lethie. 'See for yourself. No harm done, that should put your mind at rest.'

'You mean it never was stolen.'

'No. Mislaid.' And Sir Terence closed his lips firmly in the manner of one prepared to say no more on that particular subject.

Faro examined the cabinet and turning, regarded him sternly. 'I understand that this is a very valuable object of great historical importance. May I suggest that in future you keep it under lock and key as a deterrent to thieves.'

That idea had clearly never occurred to its owner. 'My dear Inspector.' Sir Terence pointed to the ancient case. 'It has hung there for, well, hundreds of years, and it has never been in any danger from thieves —'

'Times have changed, Sir Terence. As you are probably aware, crime is on the increase and we have travelled a long way from the days when lairds were regarded by their clansmen as sacrosanct and only a little lower than God.'

This particular laird clearly did not like such a reminder. 'I have to tell you, Inspector, that my tenants are one hundred per cent reliable — to the last man,' he snapped.

'Nevertheless, this suspected burglary has now been recorded in my office. Such matters are regarded as very serious offences —'

'As I told your sergeant,' Sir Terence interrupted impatiently, 'it was all a mistake. The

Luck had been removed for — for cleaning — it has since been replaced.'

'Replaced?'

'Indeed so.' Sir Terence frowned. 'I'm not quite sure how to begin.'

Faro was aware of a movement behind him. Roma Fortescue had entered the room. She was looking flushed and extremely pretty.

'Perhaps I should tell him, Terence.' And turning, she smiled at Faro. 'I took it —'

Sir Terence began to protest.

She held up her hand. 'Please — please let me explain.'

'If you would be so good, miss.'

'It's rather a long story. You see, we have a Horn of Plenty in the palace, identical to your Luck of Lethie and reputedly brought back by a band of Knights Templars who sought sanctuary with us from persecution in the thirteenth century. It was always understood, although there was no written evidence, of course, that it was part of the booty taken from King Solomon's Temple in Jerusalem and that they bequeathed it to those early rulers of Luxoria in gratitude for their hospitality.

'Our Royal Family have known poverty and hardships in the last few years, but despite pressure from the President, they have resisted any suggestions that it should be sold.'

She smiled. 'A superstitious man, knowing its reputation, he would be afraid to take it by force. What he was unaware of, however — as

217

it is a closely guarded family secret — is that two hundred years ago the Horn of Plenty disappeared, and some time later miraculously reappeared. Whatever happened to it in the interval, whether it was stolen or sold, we have no idea —'

As she spoke, Faro remembered that two hundred years ago Major Weir, the wizard of the West Bow appeared in Edinburgh, accompanied by a magic staff with a snake's head and amazing powers. Could they be one and the same?

'— This was an additional reason for this visit by Amelie,' Miss Fortescue continued, 'to find out if what we had was, in truth, the original Horn of Plenty. I'm afraid she considered that, regardless of its supposed powers, we could no longer be sentimental and that the time was now ripe for us to sell it.'

'Had you a buyer in mind?' Faro interrupted sharply.

She smiled. 'Indeed, yes. An American multimillionaire with a young wife who is childless and who knew of its legends, was very keen to possess it.'

'These supposed magic qualities,' said Faro, 'would they be altered by selling it? Surely that is the traditional belief — that such powers cannot be sold.'

Three faces turned towards him, frowning.

Miss Fortescue shrugged. 'The family and Amelie herself believed most fervently in its fertility properties, it was an assurance of the continuation of the Royal dynasty. But they can no longer afford to be sentimental, they are in dire need of financial help. And without an heir they have no security; the President's power is limitless and he wields it, since they are still popular with the people, by keeping them alive but under what is in effect permanent house arrest.'

At Lady Lethie's sharp exclamation, Miss Fortescue turned and regarded her sadly. 'Yes, they are virtually prisoners, without hope of escape unless they can buy their freedom. The President is not popular. Money might also be put to a better purpose — to raise an army and overthrow him.'

She paused. 'I have no wish to sound disloyal, but it is well-known that your Queen is not only a very sentimental old lady, she is not averse to money — and to the power money brings,' she added candidly. 'The feeling was that she might even be persuaded to intervene — politically — in our present situation.'

Miss Fortescue regarded the listeners' faces anxiously, to see if the implications of what she was hinting at were clear to them. Then with a sigh, she continued:

'I have given the matter great thought. In Amelie's continued absence and on an impulse — which I assure you she would have approved of whole-heartedly — while you were away I decided to take the Luck of Lethie to the jeweller in Edinburgh myself. You will have heard of him —'

The family name she mentioned was of international renown and they had been court jewellers for many generations.

'He studied the jewels in their setting and assured me that they were undoubtedly genuine. "This piece," he told me, "is priceless." '

And, as if in echo of Faro's warning, she looked at Sir Terence.

'He asked me how it was kept, and when I told him in a glass cabinet, he threw up his hands in horror. He said it should be kept behind bars under lock and key.'

Sir Terence darted an uncomfortable glance in Faro's direction as she continued sadly:

'I knew then what I had rather expected to find out. That what we have treasured all these years in Luxoria is a worthless imitation.'

Pausing, she looked anxiously at the Lethies. 'I do hope you understand that I was not in the least influenced by this news and that I never entertained the slightest intention of stealing the Luck of Lethie.'

Conscious of their guarded expressions, she shrugged. 'It was all very embarrassing. You would never have known of its very temporary absence if I had not been delayed by the storm and forced to take refuge —' Her glance slid off Faro — 'in Edinburgh overnight.'

Lady Lethie ran to her side and put a reassuring arm about her shoulders. 'Why didn't you tell us, Roma dear? We would have understood, wouldn't we, Terence? You should have confided in us, dear. We could have helped you.'

'I had a very good reason for silence,' said Miss Fortescue. 'Don't you see, if yours had been the imitation, then I certainly would never have told you. I would not have distressed you by destroying your family's belief in the Luck of Lethie.'

She looked at Faro, her smile odd and faintly mocking. 'Luck is so often in the mind. What we make of circumstances, don't you agree, Inspector?'

Without waiting for his reply, she turned again to the Lethies: 'At least we know now that your faith is justified and that you can go on believing in its magic.'

'We will, indeed. And we're grateful to you, aren't we, Terence?' said Lady Lethie.

Sir Terence nodded, his polite smile in Faro's direction signalling dismissal. The case was closed.

Faro stood up and said: 'I didn't come about the burglary, sir.' And to Roma Fortescue he handed the Prime Minister's letter. 'This is the reason for my visit.'

He never took his eyes off her face as she read it once, and then with a bewildered expression, read it again.

'May we know —' Sir Terence began.

'Is it something serious, my dear?' asked Lady Lethie.

Although Miss Fortescue smiled and shook her head, Faro noticed that her hands trembled ever so slightly as she read out the letter to them. Nor did he miss the anxious looks that were exchanged between the Lethies before Sir Terence cleared his throat and muttered: 'Splendid to know that your mistress is in Balmoral. And safe, too.'

Safe. There was that word again, thought Faro grimly.

'But what a journey for her to make alone,' Sir Terence continued, with a man's concern for practicalities. 'I wonder how on earth she managed it, Faro?'

'She must be a lady of great resource and courage, considering her sheltered background,' Faro replied drily.

'Oh, she is, I assure you,' said Miss Fortescue. 'She is indeed.' And to Faro: 'I presume we are leaving immediately.'

'If you please, miss, the sooner the better.'

'This time tomorrow and all will be revealed, m'dear. You will know the truth behind this little mystery,' said Terence heartily. 'No doubt, a very simple explanation.'

It was never that simple. Faro knew of old and to his cost that dealings with Royal persons could be extremely devious — and dangerous. By careful circumnavigation of the facts, they could be overly economical with the truth.

And what they called truth often turned out to be only the very tip of the iceberg.

This time tomorrow —

His growing suspicions confirmed by Roma

Fortescue's reaction to the letter, Sir Terence's words echoed in his mind. This time tomorrow, he might indeed know the whole story. If he and Miss Fortescue were still alive to hear it.

Chapter 19

Faro accepted Sir Terence's offer of a bed for the night. Arrangements made for an early start by carriage to Waverley Station next morning, Miss Fortescue and Lady Lethie departed to discuss wearing apparel. The estate factor appeared and needed his lordship's presence. Sir Terence apologized and Faro, left to his own devices, walked in the direction of Mr Stuart Millar's cottage.

There was no one at home. The cottage which had seemed warmly welcoming only days ago was deserted. The fading light of an autumn afternoon lent a touch of melancholy. Overhead rooks screeched homeward and a sudden breeze sent a flurry of dead leaves rattling down the roof.

Faro walked away thoughtfully, considering again the historian's part in this tangled web of intrigue, where no one, it seemed, spoke absolute truth about anything.

On his way back through the grounds, he stopped by the Crusader's Tomb. Regarding that face almost obliterated by wind and weather, he laid his hand on the faint outline of the cross pattée.

'If only you could talk, my friend.'

Above his head, the trees were silent now. The

first faint star glittered in that vast uncharted universe beyond the planet earth, far remote from the cares of mankind.

Roma Fortescue's words regarding the Luck of Lethie came back to him. Luck is so often in the mind. What we make of the circumstances.

Faro thought: If I were a superstitious man, I'd believe in its magic too. If its legendary powers were true, it had given unlimited power to Major Weir of the West Bow and to Bailie Lethie, who rescued it from the wizard's burning and with its help built the first Lethie Castle, ensuring prosperity for himself and his heirs. And Faro had his own reasons for acknowledging that brief magic: the strange dreams and the enchantment of those timeless sweet hours when both the Luck of Lethie and Miss Roma Fortescue were sheltering under his roof.

He returned to the castle and slept well in a very handsome modern bedroom, untroubled by the Luck of Lethie and the ghosts that had haunted generations of its owners.

Lady Lethie, who had last-minute shopping to do in Edinburgh before their departure to France, accompanied them in the carriage. Her maid sat silently at her side, giving little opportunity for any conversation other than polite trivialities.

But Faro, glancing across at Roma Fortescue, felt that she was not engrossed by urgent pleas for advice on ribbons and lace and satin gowns. He fancied that her replies were short and distracted. Her constant frowns suggested anxious preoccupation, similar to his own, with the rail journey ahead.

At the station, leaving the two women exchanging farewells and promises of letters to be written, Faro headed in the direction of the ticket office.

The queue was surprisingly long and just ahead of him he recognized Stuart Millar and his sister Elspeth, with a porter carrying their golf clubs.

They greeted him warmly. 'You are going to Perth too, Inspector?' said Elspeth.

'Just as far as Errol.'

They hovered politely while he purchased his tickets and Faro wasn't at all sure that he really wanted their company at that precise moment.

'I looked in at your house last night,' he said by way of conversation.

Millar smiled. 'We have been away for a few days to the Borders.'

'Staying with friends,' his sister put in eagerly. Trying to get in a little practice, you know.'

'I didn't realize you were golfers,' said Faro, waving to Miss Fortescue, who hurried towards them.

Millar laughed. 'Oh, yes, indeed. It is quite a vice of ours.'

Greeting Miss Fortescue, Elspeth's smile was also a question. She would have liked to know a lot more about why these two were going on this particular train, and with luggage. But before she could find the right words, she and her brother were hailed by a foursome, who announced they were keeping seats.

Faro watched them depart, and taking his companion's arm, he walked down the platform in search of an empty carriage. Many with the same idea had been there before them and they had to share a compartment, fortunate to get the two remaining seats.

'The train is unusually full,' said Faro to the four other occupants.

'The golf tournament, I expect. It's always very popular.'

Faro leaned out of the window. Among those hurrying along the platform were Vince and Leslie Godwin, with Batey in tow.

'Didn't know you were to be on this train, Stepfather. We have seats booked further along.'

Leslie hovered smiling, waiting to be introduced to Miss Fortescue. Faro, observing his cousin's admiring expression, did not miss his arch glance as he said:

'Never expected to find myself on a golfing expedition. Vince persuaded me to come along. All very mysterious, said there might be a story in it somewhere.' He grinned. 'A duel to the death on the greensward, or something of the sort, perhaps.'

As the trio prepared to move on, an elderly man puffed his way along the platform.

Sir Hedley Marsh. He did not look particularly surprised to see Miss Fortescue. Embarrassed perhaps, but not surprised.

'Are you going to the golf too, sir?' Faro asked,

guessing that was highly improbable.

'Nothing like that. Off to see one of my relatives. Family crisis and all that sort of thing.'

At the advent of Sir Hedley, Vince had seized Leslie's arm and with a despairing heavenward glance retreated down the train, with the Mad Bart in hot pursuit, much to Faro's amusement.

As the journey began, Faro stared out of the window. He had a great deal to think about and he found his companion had little to contribute. Immediately the train moved out of the station, she took out a book and held it firmly on her knee. However, each time Faro glanced in her direction, she was in fact staring bleakly out of the window. And when their eyes met, she deliberately turned a page with a frown of deep concentration. Faro had long since decided that the book was merely a protective device against any attempt at conversation — or more important, explanations.

He was relieved when the train drew in to Errol halt.

If only he could communicate with Vince. Then Faro's prayers were answered. A window opened further down the train and Vince leaned out and shouted a greeting.

The words Faro was mouthing in reply were cut short when Leslie also leaned out and waved to them, and Vince, making room for him, ducked back into the carriage.

Faro picked up Miss Fortescue's bag and regarded the departing train with considerable misgivings. He now had sufficient evidence to believe that he was walking into a trap, but there was no other way of bringing the assassin into the open.

'No train times?'

Miss Fortescue found the absence of this information less disturbing than he did. 'Don't concern yourself about that. I expect other arrangements will be made for your return to Edinburgh. Amelie and the Royal party will have arrived by carriage from Balmoral —'

It was a short walk across the grounds to Errol Towers, a handsome Georgian mansion worthy of the name of castle. Sir Piers Strathaird was famous as a racing enthusiast, and grazing in a field bordering the drive, several splendid horses from his stables trotted over to inspect these strangers and give them friendly welcome.

Roma Fortescue stopped to stroke the boldest. 'Aren't they simply beautiful?'

But Faro's attention was drawn to the battlements. The flagpole was empty. Odd that this normal indication of the laird in residence was lacking. More significant was the lack of carriages arriving and servants darting to and fro, that characteristic atmosphere of suppressed excitement and activity one would have expected of an imminent visit from Her Majesty.

Even more curious and disquieting, on closer examination, the lower windows were shuttered from the inside and the house looked deserted. He was relieved, however, to find the door promptly opened by the housekeeper, Mrs Ashley.

Inviting them to step into the hall, she announced that Sir Piers was at present with Her Majesty at Balmoral.

'The house itself,' she said, glancing over her shoulder towards open doors revealing shrouded shapes of furniture, 'is closed. The rest of the family are abroad. But the dower house across the gardens has been prepared for your visit. If you would care to follow me —'

Across rambling gardens and twisting paths, the dower house was invisible from the main house. A Scottish castle in miniature, complete with turrets, ivy-covered walls and a rustic porch. It was also very small. Faro decided uneasily that Her Majesty was keeping strictly to her word of secrecy and informality as Mrs Ashley's tour of the premises revealed only four small bedrooms.

Leaving his still-silent companion in one of them, he asked the housekeeper when the visitors from Balmoral were expected.

Mrs Ashley gave him an odd look. 'I'm not quite sure what you mean, sir. I had a telegraph telling me to have the dower house in readiness for visitors from Edinburgh — Mr Faro and a lady,' she added pointedly, unable to conceal her curiosity. And when Faro did not respond, she said quickly: 'You will be well looked after, sir. There are always an adequate number of servants —'

Faro went downstairs. The tiny house had been conscientiously prepared for their comfort. The panelled parlour was attractive with its cheerful fire, the walls adorned by antlers and sporting prints, and every available space held by stuffed animals and gamebirds in glass cases. He sniffed the air. The familiar smell of Mrs Brook's favourite beeswax was greatly in evidence, and on the highly polished floorboards, a large and ferocious-looking polarbearskin rug was further proof of Sir Piers's marksmanship.

From the direction of the kitchen, a young and nervous maid appeared to spread the table for their luncheon.

Cock-a-leekie soup, salmon en croûte, dessert and an excellent wine.

It was a meal worthy of Lethie Castle and Faro discovered that he was extremely hungry. He noticed that Miss Fortescue was imbibing rather freely. Her former sombre mood had vanished, to be replaced by lighthearted banter with a tendency to giggle and to remark with increasing frequency that meeting with her mistress was 'a great adventure'.

'We have so much to talk about,' she added with a happy sigh.

Faro did not doubt that and thought privately that he, for one, would need a great many very plausible explanations for those missing weeks. Even though he was now aware that the Grand Duchess Amelie was alive and well, such knowledge, instead of bringing reassurance, merely made the situation more sinister and bizarre.

Roma Fortescue twirled the wineglass in her fingers as she talked eagerly about Luxoria. Her attitude reminded Faro of travellers returning home who are suddenly overwhelmed with nostalgia for dear faces and familiar places. She was even expansive about Amelie's early days before the revolution.

Faro let her talk.

Occasionally she paused and looked across at him inviting exclamation or comment. These he readily supplied, his mind busy elsewhere. He did not doubt that they were in the deadliest of danger as he made careful assessment of the vulnerability of their surroundings.

The windows were small panes of glass between wooden astragals. No one could break in that way without using an axe, nor could the windows be opened from the inside. What bothered him most, however, was that in this replica of a castle, the architect had not considered a back door necessary for the dowager lady's servants, or that the elaborate front door required more than a latch for her security. Perhaps the lack of a bolt or any means of locking the door from the inside had been considered a wise precaution for any old lady who might be infirm.

The front door led directly into the sitting-room, an oak staircase giving access to the bedrooms above. The only entrance was also the only exit, he realized grimly.

The maid could not have left the house without them seeing her. She should surely have appeared to clear the table. Faro had rung the bell-pull twice without success before the chiming clock interrupted his companion's soliloquy.

'Surely they should have arrived by now?' she said anxiously.

With no wish to alarm her and on the excuse that the fire needed replenishing, he said: 'I'll get the maid to see if there's any message up at the house.'

As he hurried towards the kitchen he knew now that there was unlikely to be any message from anyone. At least not one he and Miss Fortescue would wish to hear.

He found the maid with her head resting on her arms, slumped over the kitchen table. He called to her, touched her and for one dread moment, he thought she was dead.

No, he mustn't let his imagination run away with him. Shaking her proved effective. Telling her: 'Go — at once. No, leave the dishes', he ushered her through the house, opened the front door carefully, and making sure the way ahead was safe for her and that she understood the message, he returned wearily to the sitting-room to find Miss Fortescue fast asleep.

Could it have been the wine? Surely not — then he remembered that trained as he was to avoiding alcohol during working hours, he had only taken a few sips from his glass.

'Roma,' he said to her. And then, 'Miss Fortescue.'

Still she didn't move. He spoke to her again. This time her response was immediate. Sitting bolt upright in the chair, she opened her eyes wide, yawned.

'I don't know when I've felt so sleepy at this hour of the day.' Yawning again, she said, 'Oh, do excuse me — I think I'll retire for a while. I was up and about very early this morning, you know.'

The words seemed to be dragged out of her, and stifling another yawn, her eyes closed wearily and she slumped back in her chair.

Seizing the carafe on the table, Faro poured out a full glass of water, then shook her by the shoulder. 'Drink this.'

She gave the glass a dazed look. 'I don't want any more to drink, thank you.'

Lifting her hand, he thrust the glass into it, raised it to her lips. 'It's only water. You mustn't fall asleep just now.'

'Oh, very well.' She took a few sips.

'All of it,' he commanded.

Giving him a puzzled look, she drained the glass which he seized and promptly refilled.

'And again,' he said.

She looked at him in horrified amazement. 'No —'

'You must, believe me — you must.'

'But why? — Oh, very well.'

Watching her drain the glass, Faro sat down opposite her.

'We haven't a great deal of time. It would help

if you were to tell me the truth.'

'What are you talking about? I really would like to close my eyes for a few moments, if you don't mind. You may wake me when they arrive.'

'No one is going to arrive. At least no one we would welcome,' he added grimly. 'Go on, keep drinking —'

As she did so, obediently this time, she said: 'What did you call me — I mean, when you woke me up?' When he didn't reply she protested weakly: 'I don't understand —'

'Oh, I think you understand very well — Your Highness.'

Chapter 20

Faro discovered that the truth was far more effective than glasses of water at throwing off the effects of the wine.

'You called me — Your Highness,' she whispered.

'I did.'

'But I'm —' she began, and then: 'How did you know?' she demanded indignantly.

'You gave the game away. You didn't respond to either Roma or Miss Fortescue, but when I called you Amelie, you woke up immediately.'

'I'm sorry —' she began, and he cut her short.

'I had guessed already.'

'But how?'

'Some day, if we ever have time, I'll tell you. But now, Your Highness, the truth, if you please. And all of it. Rest assured our lives may depend on it.'

She said sulkily, 'What else can I tell you, since you seem to know most of it? As Aunt Vicky's favourite god-daughter, I have a particularly privileged place. Anything I needed, any help, she wrote to me, I had only to ask. I realize that the President — my husband —' She stopped and drew breath as if the word choked her. 'As he is trying to get rid of me, flight seemed the only way I could stay alive.'

'Had you some evidence of the President's intentions?'

'He tried to poison me,' she said, and went on hurriedly. 'Aunt Vicky could use her influence, I thought. As I told you, anything that relates to poor Uncle Albert — and we were third cousins.

'My absence — or escape — had to be done secretly. I didn't want my family, who have suffered enough, to be held responsible. And as the President only visits me every four weeks or so, I felt I had enough time to make the visit and return without his knowledge.'

'Where did the Luck of Lethie come into all this?' Faro asked, hastily banishing a suddenly vivid picture of 'Miss Fortescue' lying in his arms.

'I had some naïve idea that it might restore our good fortune.' She sighed. 'All that I told you about its history is true. And had it been the original, then I would have been prepared to sell it to the American millionaire. I realize I behaved foolishly —'

'Impulsively — and in character,' Faro suggested, smiling.

'We had one person we could trust to make the arrangements. Roma's father, Miles Fortescue. He alerted the Lethies to the purpose of our journey —'

'So they knew who you were.'

She shook her head. 'Not at first. Had to tell

237

them. A nuisance. That day you came on us at the Crusader's Tomb. I was trying to persuade them not to make matters more complicated.' Pausing, she smiled at him. 'They suspected everyone — including you.

'Roma's father will be so relieved to know that she is safe. I have been terrified that something dreadful had happened to her. She was not at all well on the voyage, but she was determined to accompany me, despite her doctor's orders.'

'She was ill?'

'Not exactly ill, but delicate. She suffered from a heart condition — brought about by a childhood attack of rheumatic fever. Despite her frail health, she must have made that incredible journey to Balmoral Castle, alone. And, on my behalf, arranged this meeting. I'll be grateful to her for the rest of my life.'

Without suggesting that the rest of her life might not be long, Faro had now before him the melancholy business of breaking the news that the real Miss Fortescue, far from being in Balmoral, had died of a heart attack on the night of the carriage accident. Sparing her the details, he said that with no knowledge of her identity, she had been buried in Edinburgh.

Amelie was deeply distressed. 'She was so afraid that I might be kidnapped or that somehow the President might have learned of our plan. She insisted we change clothes — and jewellery — everything by which I could be identified, on the ship. When I told her she was being ridiculous and overdramatizing the situation, she just smiled and said: "Oh, they'll soon let me go when they find they've got the wrong one." '

She paused and then sobbed. 'And she's the one who is dead. Oh, dear God, I can't bear it.'

Rather awkwardly, Faro put an arm about her shoulders. It was one thing comforting a lady-in-waiting, quite another offering comfort which might be misunderstood by a Grand Duchess.

'In an unknown grave. Oh, no —' She wept at that. 'My poor Roma. When we get back, we must arrange a proper funeral —'

'Of course, of course we will.'

She dried her tears at last and raising her head, gave him a startled look. 'But then who — who is with the Queen?'

'No one, I'm afraid,' he said.

'What do you mean — no one?'

'The letter was a ruse to get you out of Edinburgh.'

'The Prime Minister —'

'A forgery. There isn't time now to tell you, but I beg you, have no illusions, you were brought to this destination with me — for one purpose only. I think you know what that purpose is,' he added grimly. 'You're a brave woman, Your Highness.'

'If you've known — what was intended, then why did you come with me?' she asked softly.

'All part of my line of duty to protect a Royal personage.'

'Is that all?' she asked softly, and in her eyes he saw reflected gratitude and something more than gratitude. Leaning over, he kissed her very gently. For a moment, she clung to him —
'Hush!'
There was a sound outside.
A wisp of smoke curled under the door.
The nightmare had begun.

Faro knew that by opening the door he presented a ready target. But from the small windows it was impossible to see who might be waiting in the porch. The smell of smoke, however, painted a grim picture of their assailant's intentions.

Amelie grabbed his arm. 'Fire — they are setting fire to the house. Don't you understand? Do something, please — for God's sake.'

He heard the panic in her voice, remembered her story of a fire in a hotel which, perhaps, had been true after all.

She watched wide-eyed as Faro took a gun from his valise and opened the door an inch. Clouds of choking smoke billowed in. Closing it hastily, he had seen enough to realize his worst fears. Their attacker had set fire to the rustic porch which would soon spread to the door.

'Get water,' he said. Amelie fled to the kitchen, returning at last with a bucket.

'All I could find,' she gasped. 'Hidden away behind a rail of maids' uniforms. We're lucky to have running water.' And with rising panic in her voice: 'There is no back door. Did you know that?'

Faro didn't doubt that whoever waited outside, also knew. Telling her to stay out of range, he opened the door and flung the water over blazing wood.

As the flames subsided, smoke gushed through and set them coughing. But there was worse than smoke now to contend with. Faro heard a sharp crack as a bullet hit the stone lintel of the door, narrowly missing him.

He fired at the moving shadow on the edge of the grass. The shadow jerked like a puppet. He heard an exclamation and realized he had hit his target.

Amelie peered over his shoulder. 'Well done. You managed it. We're safe.'

'Oh no, we're not. He wasn't alone. Listen.'

'Father — father —' The voice was Vince's. 'Come quickly.' A scream — and silence.

Amelie stared at him. 'That was Vince. You must go to him. He's been hurt. I'll be all right.'

Faro turned, handed her the gun. 'Can you use this?'

She smiled mockingly. 'I've been through a revolution. Of course I can use a gun — and anything else it takes to stay alive,' she added. 'Now go —'

Opening the door a fraction, he turned and said: 'Shoot to kill. Remember it's you they want, not me.'

'What about you — you're unarmed?'

'I can still use my fists. Don't worry about me.'

As he ran lightly across the grass, his main concern was for his stepson. It hadn't been Vince calling, of that he was sure. Although it sounded like his voice, the lad never called him anything but 'Stepfather'.

In the shrubbery he almost fell across a body. He thought at first it was Vince. It was Batey, shot in the shoulder and leaning against a tree. Realizing he had hit his target but not fatally, Faro snatched up his gun and, followed by Batey's curses, ran swiftly back towards the house.

The sudden dimness of the interior blinded him. With relief, he saw Vince stagger forward apparently unharmed. But Vince was not alone. From the shadows behind him, a voice —

'You have a choice, Jeremy. Your stepson or Her Highness.'

The smiling face was that of his cousin, Leslie Faro Godwin.

But where was Amelie?

Chapter 21

Although all the evidence had indicated the assassin's identity, Faro's heart had resolutely refused to accept what his head knew to be true. To the bitter end, he hoped that some miracle would prove his growing suspicions regarding his cousin to be false.

He watched in a daze of unbelief, Vince struggling. 'Damn you, Godwin. Damn you.'

But Leslie held him in an iron grip. 'Throw down your gun, Jeremy. You won't be needing that.' As Faro put the gun on the table, Leslie pointed to a chair. 'And do sit down, if you please. On your feet, you make me feel nervous —'

Faro did as he was told and playing for time he asked: 'Why? Just tell me why?'

Leslie laughed. 'Can't you guess? Money, my dear fellow, always money. Lost heavily in the casino in Luxoria, thrown into jail. Then the President's highly efficient intelligence service hinted that all would be forgiven if I obliged them — in a certain matter. There's no need to look like that. It isn't the first time.' He paused, then added slowly: 'You should know that by now.'

Allowing that information to sink in, he continued: 'If you want to believe in my reputation, then accept that it is only a very small step from killing a man you don't know or hate on a bat-tlefield, risking your life for nothing but glory, to killing a man — or a woman —' he emphasized grimly, 'who is someone else's deadly foe. And being handsomely paid for your trouble.

'While I was at the planning stage, I was housed here as a guest at one of Sir Piers's shooting parties. I saw the unique and admirable possi-bilities the dower house presented with the family abroad.

'Incidentally, Amelie was followed all the way from Luxoria and Batey rode out to meet them when they landed at North Berwick. He managed to arrange the accident despite that cursed storm. Amelie died (or so we believed) most obligingly, of fright. Not a hand laid on her.

'And all the time while I was at the regimental dinner being reunited with my cousin Inspector Faro, Batey — with the help of the Hogans and Sandy Dunnock — arranged for the body of Her Highness, with nothing to identify her, to be found in the Wizard's House. So that there could be no connection, the drowned coachman was to be hidden in Mrs Dunnock's closet — for a day or two. Mrs Dunnock got upset after that, complained that the smell was upsetting them.

'But where was Miss Fortescue? That worried me, but Batey assured me he'd seen her roll down into the water. Anyway, I was overcome with curiosity. I had to be certain my mission was successful before claiming my bounty. But when I followed you into the Wizard's House, I realized we had got the wrong woman. Same colouring, age and so forth. Batey's fault, but understandable in the dark with a storm raging. However, as far as we were concerned they were all dead, with two of the three bodies accounted for.'

He stopped and smiling, pointed at Faro. 'And then you, Jeremy, most obligingly, told me that Miss Fortescue was at Lethie Castle. I knew I had to work fast after that. Damned nuisance.' The smile was replaced by a scowl.

'So Batey broke into Wrightson's study and stole the headed notepaper from Holyrood —'

Leslie grinned, his charming self once more. 'He did. Wrightson had bragged about his drawer of Royal mementoes, that evening before you arrived. Another of Batey's modest accomplishments, which alas has put him behind bars in the past, is being a damned good forger. I hope he doesn't die out there. You'll be to blame. I had to leave him, the urgent need for more important quarry.'

As if remembering, he held the gun at Vince's head. 'And what have you done with Her Highness? I shall count to three and if she doesn't appear, then you can say goodbye to Vince. One — two —'

'Put down your gun.' A bespectacled uniformed maid in large white cap and apron, stood in the doorway leading from the kitchen holding Faro's gun. The voice with its unmistakable note of authority was Amelie's.

Unperturbed, Leslie laughed. 'Ah, I'm slipping.

A terrified maid busy at the kitchen sink, wrestling with steaming pans. Who ever would have suspected that Her Highness would stoop so low —'

'I said, put down your gun.'

Leslie shook his head. Shielded by Vince's body, he knew he had won. 'Too late, madam. Hand it to me — or Vince will die.'

Amelie looked hard at Faro and held out the gun at an angle so that Leslie had to turn slightly towards her. The momentary diversion of his attention was enough. Leslie's feet were on the bearskin rug. Knowing what was at stake if he failed, in one swift movement, Faro slid the chair along the polished floor. Swooping down, he grabbed the rug — and tugged.

'What the devil —'

Leslie, holding Vince as shield, was thrown off balance. Vince fell hard against him and twisting round, tried to seize the gun. As they struggled, it slithered across the floor and they both cannoned into Amelie, who was also knocked off her feet, her gun spinning towards Faro.

Seizing it, his finger on the trigger he levelled it at Leslie. But he knew that whatever the cost, he could not kill his cousin like this, at close range.

And Leslie read his mind. Smiling, he bowed slightly. 'I am unarmed, as you see.' Turning he leaped through the open door. Faro followed him shouting:

'Come on, Vince —'

Vince started forward, then with an exclamation of pain: 'I can't, Stepfather. I twisted my ankle out there —'

'Look after Amelie —' Faro could move quickly but his cousin was even quicker. Pursuing him through the thick vegetation of trees and shrubbery, at last he emerged on the drive.

As he looked round, one of Sir Piers's racehorses jumped over the railings and galloped towards the gates, Leslie riding bareback.

Faro watched him go, cursing. An indifferent horseman at the best of times, he knew that pursuit was useless. Winded, breathless he headed back to the dower house, to be overtaken by a troop of mounted policemen from Perth.

'Get after him.' But he knew it was already too late.

In the kitchen, Mrs Ashley sat at the table opposite the Perth detective, overlooked by Vince and Amelie.

'. . . and when my Davey, the local constable, came in for his supper, I told him about this Mr and Mrs Faro. Mollie thought there was something very sinister about the pair of them too.'

All heads turned in the direction of the maid who had served lunch at the dower house. This was her moment of glory.

'Aye, there was that — especially *him.*'

Inspector Macrae of the Perth Constabulary sprang to his feet as Faro entered. He didn't know how much he had overheard but had the grace to look embarrassed knowing Faro's reputation with the Edinburgh City Police.

'We were never alerted about any Royal arrival,' he told him. 'I'm glad we got here in time to avert a tragedy. Dr Laurie was telling me —'

Faro smiled wryly. They had been too late. The drama was over and they had already lost their man. But Vince was still alive and so was Amelie.

'There's a wounded man out there,' he said, and Vince limped towards the clearing. But Batey, like his master, had disappeared without trace.

Perth Constabulary provided an escort to accompany Amelie, Grand Duchess of Luxoria, on her journey to Balmoral.

For Faro, seeing her into the carriage, this was a formal farewell. As they clasped hands briefly and he solemnly wished her godspeed, there was for an instant reflected in their eyes, the sad certainty that they were unlikely ever to meet again.

Worse than any parting with the woman he would always think of as Roma Fortescue was Faro's disillusion regarding Leslie Faro Godwin. Vince, whose first instinct about Godwin had proved to be the right one, realized how deeply his stepfather was shocked by the discovery that his cousin was a hired assassin.

Over and over, Faro asked himself — and Vince — where lay the difference between them? Was his own role as a detective merely one other facet of the same violence that erupted in Leslie Faro

Godwin, making one man fight on the side of law and order and the other, of his own blood, into a hired killer?

And painfully he came to realize that the margin was very narrow indeed, as he remembered how uncovering the riddle of his father's death, he had learned that the highest and noblest in the land were far from incorruptible.

But the surprises, however, weren't over.

While Faro wondered how he could spare his mother the awful revelations about her nephew, a letter came from Orkney in reply to his glowing account of their first meeting after many years.

'I don't know what you're on about,' he read. 'Whoever this man is who calls himself Leslie Faro Godwin, he certainly isn't a relative of ours. Your cousin Leslie took scarlet fever and died just weeks after your dear father's funeral. We were just back in Orkney. You loved Leslie and we tried to tell you but you just wouldn't — or couldn't — take it in. You were only four and suffering bad dreams over your poor father —'

And Faro paused, remembering that childish nightmare of his hero cousin and his father carried away from him by a carriage with black horses.

'— You never spoke his name again. Neither did I, God forgive me —'

Faro put down the letter.

'Grandma wouldn't know about a war correspondent, would she?' said Vince. 'Then who on earth was this Leslie Faro Godwin?'

'I don't know, lad, but I intend to find out.'

His enquiries revealed that there was indeed a war correspondent called Leslie Godwin. All his exploits were quite correct. Alive and well, he lived mostly in America with his wife and children. At the time of his impostor's sojourn in Scotland, he was at the White House, receiving an award from the President of the United States.

Faro found the audacity of his counterfeit cousin deeply disturbing. It suggested an association of assassins readily available and funded by an international society which Faro had long suspected lay at the root of many unexplained and unsolved murders. A secret society with origins older and deadlier than the respectable Freemasons to which so many merchants and upper-class citizens were proud to belong.

The case of the missing Duchess had still one more card to play.

Winter came, the year turned, spring bloomed and summer blossomed, and found Faro once again involved in his daily business of solving another series of crimes.

One day, a small paragraph in *The Scotsman* drew his immediate attention.

'Heir for Luxoria: After many years of marriage to President Gustav, Her Highness the Grand Duchess Amelie has given birth to an heir. Born prematurely, despite fears for his survival, the babe shows every sign of being a strong healthy infant.'

A week later, Faro received a letter with a Luxorian stamp. In it a copy of the announcement. Underneath, in ink, the words:

'*We* have a son. Gratefully, RF.'

Author's Note

References to Faro's investigation of his policeman father's death (on page 13 and elsewhere) are from *Bloodline*, one of his first three cases to be included (with *Enter Second Murderer* and *Deadly Beloved*) in a Pan paperback omnibus edition, *Inspector Faro and the Edinburgh Mysteries*, to be published in December 1994.

We hope you have enjoyed this Large Print book. Other G.K. Hall & Co. or Chivers Press Large Print books are available at your library or directly from the publishers. For more information about current and upcoming titles, please call or write, without obligation, to:

G.K. Hall & Co.
P.O. Box 159
Thorndike, Maine 04986
USA
Tel. (800) 223-6121 (U.S. & Canada)
In Maine call collect: (207) 948-2962

OR

Chivers Press Limited
Windsor Bridge Road
Bath BA2 3AX
England
Tel. (0225) 335336

All our Large Print titles are designed for easy reading, and all our books are made to last.